THE NON-STATISTICAL MAN

By
RAYMOND F. JONES

ARMCHAIR FICTION
PO Box 4369, Medford, Oregon 97504

*For more information about Armchair Books and products, visit our
website at...*

www.armchairfiction.com

Or email us at...

armchairfiction@yahoo.com

HUMAN INTUITION IN A PILL?

Charles Bascomb was a man of precise logic—not too surprising he pushed facts and figures for a big insurance company. Every thought he had, every action he took, was based on his steadfast, nearly religious belief in the accuracy of numbers and statistics.

But something was amiss. How was it possible that a select group of people seemed to have a power of intuition greater than the essence of pure logic itself? How was it possible that, with nothing more than a hunch to go on, they all seemed to have the foresight of knowing the exact moment in time when they should purchase an insurance policy? It was a maddening riddle for a man who had spent his whole life anchored in reason, cause, and effect. Soon this baffling mystery would lead to an eccentric doctor and his little bottles of multi-colored pills.

FOR A SECOND COMPLETE NOVEL, TURN TO PAGE 107

CAST OF CHARACTERS

CHARLES BASCOMB
If you needed a numbers man he was your guy! But what if all your numbers, statistics and logic were…well…wrong?

SARAH BASCOMB
Her husband thought she was an illogical scatterbrain. But when he ran the numbers on her "feelings"…she was most often right!

HADLEY
He was a man-on-the-rise, and his efforts to impress his superiors would set the world of statistics on its ear.

DR. MAGRUDER
What were his true intentions with the little colored pills he handed out so easily?

MARK SLOANE
Nothing like some good old capitalistic know how, and his product was packaged perfectly—but why wouldn't it sell?

HAP JOHNSON
The firestorm this reporter started was impressive. But it wasn't quite the storm his pal Charlie had expected.

ZAD CLEMENTI
Was he really guilty of murder? That simple question could set the wheels of one man's destruction into motion!

CHAPTER ONE

CHARLES BASCOMB was a man who loved figures—the genuine, Arabic kind, that is. Not that he didn't adequately appreciate the other kind, too. Mrs. Bascomb was quite good in that department, but Charles had come to take her somewhat for granted after fourteen years of married life—plus three young Bascombs who had taught him what a great obligation can be implied by so small a number.

Bascomb considered himself a realist, and pointed to his passion for figures to prove it. If an opinion were given—whether on the price of hamburger in Denver or the difference between the climate of his hometown of Landbridge, and that of Los Angeles, California—he demanded figures and odds.

Yet, in his world of endlessly marching columns of black numerals, there was escape, too. It was clean and cold and precise here. The scatterbrained effusions and emotionalism of Sarah Bascomb were lacking. Charles Bascomb loved his wife, but she was scatterbrained. And the utterly irrational demands of the small Bascombs could not penetrate.

All irrationality was swept aside, and here, and here alone, could be had a clear view of the real world. It would have been difficult for Bascomb to say if the question had been put to him, which was the real world and which was fairyland. Mrs. Bascomb and the kids were real enough—in their place—but they couldn't possibly fit in the realm of precise figures, which was the *real* world.

Fortunately, no one ever asked Mr. Bascomb about this, and it was never pushed into his awareness beyond an occasional fuzzy, gnawing feeling that there should be more congruity between these two areas than there was.

It was generally quite deliciously satisfying to him to know that he could tell, for example—with almost perfect accuracy—how many of the citizens he passed on the street on the way to the station each night would not be alive by the end of the year. He could tell almost precisely how many would be alive in another five years, provided he had their present ages, of course. And he could tell how many would die of diabetes, and heart trouble, and cancer.

There was a satisfaction in knowing these things. There was a satisfaction in his work of assembling such information and producing the proper deductions. (He was Chief Statistical Analyst of the New England Mutual Cooperative Insurance Company.) There was a sense of power in it.

But Bascomb believed he was a humble man. The power was in the figures, in the statistical methods which constituted the temple wherein he but served as priest.

At the age of thirty-seven he believed he would serve his god of figures for the remainder of his life. And, certainly, on that morning of April tenth, when one of the Junior Statisticians came to his office, he considered himself safe and secure in the groove he would run in until he himself became a statistic in the Company's books.

BASCOMB looked up and smiled pleasantly as Hadley approached his desk—there was no reason for being otherwise.

"Good morning, Hadley," he said. "You look as if the weekend treated you well. Mrs. Hadley get over her cold all right?"

"She's fine, Mr. Bascomb." Hadley was a youngster, still in his first year of marriage. He shared Bascomb's passion for figures—Arabic—and hoped to rise high in the firm. Hadley spread out some long sheets of paper and bent over the desk. "We ran across something interesting last week that I thought I'd like to show you. I've never seen anything like this before."

"What is it?" said Bascomb.

"District reports of claims in Division 3 show some curious anomalies. In the town of Topworth, we had eighteen claims registered on all types of policies and—"

"That is not an unusual number for a town of that size."

"No—but here's the catch. Those policies had been taken out less than six weeks ago, with only two exceptions. Now, here in Burraston we have nine claims—all on policies less than six weeks old, no exceptions. And in Victorburg—"

"Let me see that!"

Bascomb drew the sheets toward him and adjusted the heavy, shell-framed glasses that seemed to grip the sides of his head rather than rest on his ears.

"In Victorburg—twenty seven claims on policies only four weeks old." He ripped the glasses away from his face and looked up. "How large is Victorburg, Hadley?"

"Only thirty-two thousand, Mr. Bascomb." He waited, knowing he'd said enough for the moment.

BASCOMB bit the tip of the earpiece on his glasses and looked down again. He rustled the wide sheets of paper. "This is one of the strangest things I have seen since I've been in the insurance business," he said. "We know that in statistics we sometimes encounter long runs of an anomalous nature, but three cities like this—"

"There are seven altogether," said Hadley. "I went back and checked over some of our more recent records in the same district. The other four are less pronounced—six to eight each—but they are there."

"Very strange, to say the least," said Mr. Bascomb mildly now. "I think I'd like very much to follow up the details and see if any explanation can be found—beyond merely assigning it as an unusual run."

"I have all the claim papers on my desk."

"Get me the initial applications also. Was there any consistency shown in the salesmen who wrote the policies?"

"No. About a dozen different salesmen are involved. The only pertinent factor I've found is that in these last three towns we have new agencies, which have put on a big campaign backed by our national advertising. But that doesn't explain, of course, why they should have written policies on which claims were to be made so quickly."

"No, of course not; get me all the papers available."

BASCOMB spent the rest of the morning computing the normal claims expectancy for each of the towns involved. He figured the probabilities of encountering such runs as had come up; he examined in detail the applications of all the policyholders.

On the death claims there was the usual medical certification showing the applicants to be in acceptable health at time of policy writing. Two had died of polio; one in a car accident; four of coronary trouble—that should have been caught! There were two cancer cases—they should have been found, too. Some of the trouble was evidently in the medical department; he'd see that some overhauling was done there.

But blaming the examiners would not dispose of the whole problem, by any means; the accident and liability claims could not be dismissed so easily. There was only one factor of any significance, which he was able to discover. Better than ninety percent of the applications had come in through voluntary response to the company's advertising. They hadn't been sold by the usual foot-in-the-door salesman Bascomb so thoroughly disapproved of.

That would be worth noting to the sales department!

But, on the other hand, had their advertising suddenly become so much better? He called the advertising manager and asked for copies of whatever displays had been available in the seven towns during the period the policies were sold.

He was interrupted then by some current items that killed the better part of the afternoon. When he finally got around to the advertisements, it was almost time to quit. It would be too rough if he missed the five-seventeen—there would be time enough to get back to this problem tomorrow.

Yet, that would not do, either; there was something too persistently nagging about this, too many "queer" aspects to let the matter alone even overnight. He broke a long-standing rule between him and Sarah Bascomb, and stuffed the entire mass of papers into his briefcase to take home.

SARAH BASCOMB was well aware that she didn't live in the same world with her husband, and that made it rather nice, she thought. It would have been exceedingly boring if they *both* talked of nothing but expectancy tables and statistical probabilities, or the PTA and young Chuck's music lessons.

As it was, she thought they got along fine. She listened with honest attentiveness to Charles' discussions of the ratio of cancer to coronary deaths, and the increase of both over pneumonia and other infectious diseases during the past thirty years. It was so boring as to be absolutely incredible; but she was thankful that there were men like Charles in the world to take care of these particular things—which had to be taken care of, but which no ordinary person would think of concerning himself with.

She was proud of Charles' ability to deal with such obscure and unpleasant material, and she listened to it because she was in love with him. It didn't occur to her that it was in any way disloyal to feel it was all very stuffy.

In turn, Charles took an active interest in household affairs—and left all the answers up to her, which was the way she liked it. It would have been intolerable if he'd been one of those men who insist on planning the dinner menu, or picking the kids' dentist, or seeing Mr. Salers down the street when Chuck and the Salers kid had an after-school knock-down, drag-out argument.

Sarah was quite willing and able to take care of these items alone. At thirty-five she was a competent, contented, still good-looking suburban housewife without a cloud on the domestic horizon.

But on this particular April tenth she had been a trifle uneasy all day. There was the feeling that momentous things were about to happen to disturb the complacency of Charles' life and hers. She often had such feelings and Charles told her they were ridiculous; but over the years, Sarah had sort of kept track of them. She'd discovered that these feelings always meant something, one way or another—especially when they were this strong.

So she was not surprised to see the brief case in Charles' hand as she watched him from the kitchen window, coming through the breezeway to the house.

SHE TURNED, as if she hadn't seen him, and attended to the noisy sputtering frying of his favorite—liver with onions. She squealed with simulated surprise and pleasure as his arms came about her waist, and he kissed her on the back of the neck.

Then she pretended to notice the bulging briefcase for the first time. "Big business tonight? I thought maybe we could go out to a show at the Centre—?"

Bascomb smiled, shrugged a little, and tossed the briefcase carelessly to a chair across the room. "Nothing very important; just a little problem that came up today—but it can wait. We'll see the show if you want to. What's on?"

Sarah shook her head. "Nothing in particular; it's not that important. I want you to spend the evening on your problem. That is important. And I want you to tell me all about it."

They settled the problem, as Sarah knew they would, by staying home. And after dinner, she sat very quietly and attentively while Charles tried to explain why it was upsetting to come across such a run of events as had turned up. Try as she would, however, Sarah could not quite grasp the significance of it, or the reason for astonishment.

"You say it might be expected to happen once in a few hundred centuries," she insisted, "so I should think you'd be glad the time is now, when you are able to witness it."

BASCOMB smiled with tolerance; there was no use trying to make her understand. "It's just that a fellow doesn't expect to be around for the event," he said. "We talk about it, and use it in our figuring; but we just don't expect to see it."

"That's what makes it all the more exciting!" Sarah's eyes were alight in a way she hoped would make Charles think she understood what he was talking about.

Then her expression grew more somber. "And I think it's something terribly important, too," she said. "I feel that it's something which could mean a great deal to our future, Charles. I *know* it. Tell me as soon as you find out what it really means."

Bascomb muttered a growl of exasperation in the bottom of his throat. This was the kind of thing that came close to driving him to distraction—Sarah's "feelings" that something-or-other was going to happen, or was especially meaningful.

It gave him the shudders when she started talking that way—because the most damnable part was that she was often right. He had started keeping check on it, out of pure self-defense, a long time ago. Her batting average gave him a queasy feeling in the pit of his stomach.

"There's nothing significant for us in this crazy thing," he said irritably. "It's just a bunch of policies that came up for claim all at once—when our statistical methods gave us no reason to expect it. That's absolutely all; it's ridiculous, darling, to try to read anything more in it."

"You'll tell me, won't you?" Sarah Bascomb said.

CHARLES accomplished nothing toward a solution of the problem that night. At the end of four hours' work, it seemed just as inexplicable as it did when Brooks first mentioned it.

He slept badly, his line of disturbed thought alternating between the problem itself and Sarah's irrational interpretation of its significance. In the morning he arose and told himself that it was idiotic to allow a small, routine problem of this kind to get so out of hand.

Only it wasn't small, and it wasn't routine by any means.

As he sipped his coffee across the breakfast table from Sarah, and with the three youngsters beginning to stir noisily overhead, he said cautiously, "I've been thinking that it might almost be worthwhile to have a personal interview with these policyholders, and see if anything can be deduced from firsthand contact with them. Of course, it's silly to hope for anything definite, but I think maybe I'll do it."

He held his coffee cup poised while he waited for her answer. And now *he* was the idiot, he thought—as if her opinion could be of any possible significance!

Nevertheless, Bascomb waited, head cocked to catch the slightest inflection of her voice.

"I think that's the most sensible thing you've done about the whole problem," she said. "After all, who could tell you more about why they bought the policies when they did—and how they came to make claims—than the people themselves?"

That cinched it, and Charles Bascomb fumed at himself for asking the question of Sarah. After all, he'd intended doing just this, anyway, hadn't he? What difference did her uninformed opinion make to him? But then, her comment was a good one; who, indeed, could tell more about the purchase of these policies than the people who'd done the buying?

He called the office and told his assistant, Jarvis, what he was doing and gave him instructions for carrying on.

CHAPTER TWO

OF THE SEVEN towns, Victorburg was closest to Landbridge, so Charles Bascomb started for there, feeling unfamiliar in heading the car onto the open highway instead of driving to the station. He congratulated himself that these cases had turned up close to the Home Office, instead of halfway across the United States; at the same time, Bascomb told himself once more he was a complete idiot for giving the whole thing this much attention.

He reached Victorburg by ten o'clock, and drove at once to the first address on his list. It was a quiet, tree-shaded street that added to the peacefulness of the April morning. He pulled up in front of a neat, white frame house.

Mrs. Davidson; she was the claimant on one of the death cases—Mr. Davidson had died of coronary trouble just three weeks ago. Bascomb wondered if he shouldn't have gone first to one of the lesser claimants. But it was too late, now. A woman working in the garden at the side of the house had seen him; she was looking up. He got out of the car with his briefcase in his hand.

He tipped his hat as he came up. "Mrs. Davidson? I'm a representative of the New England Mutual Cooperative."

The woman's face showed instant dismay. "Oh, dear—I hope there's nothing wrong now. Your payment came through so quickly, and I was able to pay—"

"No, no—there's nothing wrong," Mr. Bascomb said hastily. "Just a routine check we always make to determine if the policyholder has been entirely satisfied with our service."

"Oh, yes! It's been more than satisfactory," exclaimed Mrs. Davidson. "Your payment came through so promptly, and I don't know what we would have done without it. John went so suddenly, you know. It seems like a miracle that we thought of taking out insurance on him just before it happened. He'd always been so violently opposed to insurance all his life, you know—never would consider it until just now, when it was so badly needed. We didn't know it was going to be needed, of course."

"OF COURSE," said Bascomb. "Our medical examiner passed Mr. Davidson as being in good health at the time of application; otherwise the policy could not have been issued.

"We share your feelings of gratitude that you were fortunate enough to have the policy in force at the time of Mr. Davidson's illness. And so you feel you are satisfied with the service our company has given you?"

"Indeed I do!"

"It seems strange there was no earlier indication of your husband's condition. Hadn't he ever noticed it before?"

"Never. He was always so strong and healthy; that's why he despised insurance salesmen so—said they always made him feel as if he were going to die next week."

"But he *did* finally change his mind. That is the thing I am most interested in, Mrs. Davidson. You see, we realize we have a service of positive value to offer people; but sometimes, as in the case of your husband, we simply have no means of making them understand it. So naturally, we are most interested to know what finally breaks down a great prejudice against us. You would be doing us a great favor if you could help us in presenting better appeals to other people."

"I see what you mean, but I don't know how I could help you. It just seemed like the thing to do; both John and I felt that way about the same time. It just seemed to be the thing to do."

Mr. Bascomb felt a trifle numb for a moment. There seemed to be a coldness in the air he hadn't noticed before. It was as if Sarah were there, standing in front of him.

"You just *felt* like taking out some insurance?" he said faintly.

Mrs. Davidson nodded. "I don't suppose that's much help, is it? But it's the best I can do, I'm afraid. Surely you know how those things are, though? You get a hunch something ought to be done, without knowing why. That's the way it was with us. I know it seems silly to most people, but I believe in hunches—don't you, Mr. Bascomb?"

Bascomb felt that he had to get away quickly. He nodded and picked up the briefcase from the grass where he'd dropped it. "Yes, I do," he said, backing toward the street. "Hunches are invaluable—especially in matters of this kind!"

HE DROVE partway around the block, and stopped to consider. He was irritated with himself for his reaction to Mrs. Davidson's talk. What had he expected? A profound self-analysis as to just why she, as a customer of New England, had chosen that particular policy? Or, rather, why her husband had?

He'd probably get even more of the same kind; it's what you had to take when dealing with individuals. That was why statistics had to be invented—because people were so unstable and irrational, taken one at a time.

Bascomb wished that he could forget the whole thing right now. But he couldn't; his encounter with Mrs. Davidson had only convinced him that there must be an absolutely sound statistical explanation for the run of short policy claims. He started the car and drove to the next address on his list, three blocks away.

THINGS were better here; the customer was a young physician who had just opened up a small, neighborhood clinic. He had made a liability claim when a patient stumbled on a hose lying across the walk.

"I always feel it necessary to be protected this way," he said amiably to Bascomb's question. His name was Dr. Rufus Sherridan. "It's the only sensible way to look at it."

"Absolutely," agreed Bascomb; "it's the thing we've been trying for years to drum into the heads of the public. Be protected. Juries act as if they're crazy nowadays when they hand out somebody else's money in a damage suit."

"As to my making a substantial claim within three weeks of paying my first premium—well, that's why we have insurance companies, isn't it?" said Dr. Sherridan, smiling. "I was never able to understand the figures and statistics of how you work these things out, but the idea is to spread the risk of such unfortunate coincidences, is it not?"

"That's it exactly," said Mr. Bascomb. "Well, it's been a pleasure to meet you, Doctor." He extended a hand. "I hope you will always find our service as satisfactory as it was this time."

"I'm sure I shall; thank you for calling," said Dr. Sherridan.

Bascomb had hoped to contact all twenty-seven cases in Victorburg in one day; by five o'clock, however, he had reached only number eighteen. Most of them had been somewhere between Mrs. Davidson and Dr. Sherridan, and Bascomb was exhausted. He longed for his desk and his figures, the world where he knew what was going on.

NUMBER eighteen turned out to be the worst of all, a considerable number of notches below Mrs. Davidson. She was willing to *talk* for one thing; it took Bascomb almost twenty minutes to get to his critical question.

"Why did we decide at this particular time to buy a policy with your company?" Her name was Mrs. Harpersvirg, and she had a habit of putting her arms akimbo and fixing him with narrowed eyes, head cocked sharply to one side.

"We knew we were going to need it, Mr. Bascomb. That's why we bought a policy. Oh, I know you'll say a person can't know those things, and it's true for most people. But once you learn how to realize what's the right and proper action to take under any circumstance, it's just like getting a breath of really fresh air for the first time in your life."

Bascomb leaned back on his heels as she edged toward him. "You have come to such an understanding, Mrs. Harpersvirg?" he asked tentatively.

"You bet! And all I can say is, it's wonderful! You don't have to grovel around with your nose in the mud, wondering where you're going and what's going to happen next and what you ought to do about it. You can *do* something about it. Of course, I didn't believe it when Dr. Magruder said it would be that way; but the way this insurance policy paid off convinced me once and for all. I'm glad you called, Mr. Bascomb. I've got to rush now. You can tell your company we're very happy with their service!"

She banged away and left Mr. Bascomb standing there struggling with his final question: who was Dr. Magruder?

But it was obviously of no importance—probably he was some semi-quack family practitioner in the neighborhood. Bascomb turned and almost fled toward the sanctuary of his car; Mrs. Harpersvrig was the final straw in a day that would exhaust the best of men.

And then, somewhere along the seventy-five mile drive back home, it hit Bascomb like a rabbit punch in a dark alley. The common factor.

IN STATISTICS you look for the common factor in order to lump otherwise dissimilar items in a single category. And the common factor here was that each of the policyholders he'd interviewed claimed to have bought in with New England on the basis of a hunch-intuition. From Mrs. Harpersvrig on up to Dr. Sherridan—well, maybe the Doctor could be excepted, but certainly none of the others could.

No high-pressure sales talk had sold them; they weren't attracted by more than cursory interest in the company's fancy literature and advertising. They had bought simply because they'd felt it the thing to do; almost every one of them had used nearly those exact words.

Intuition—a random factor that ordinarily made no impression on statistical analysis.

These people were making it work!

Bascomb slowed the car at the impact of the thought. He finally pulled off to the side of the road to check his interview notes. The damning words were repeated in every possible variation, but they were there:

"We just figured it was time we ought to have some insurance."

"It's hard to say—I guess we were just impressed to buy when we did."

"I don't know. I felt it was the thing we needed as soon as I heard your company was opening an office here."

Bascomb closed the book shakily, and resumed driving—slowly. It was tempting to jump to conclusions in a thing like this, but that was absolutely the thing you couldn't do. There was really no basis for assigning a positive correlation between the short policy claims and the intuitive purchasing by the holders. That was the kind of thing on which a man could trip himself up badly; and he certainly wasn't going to fall into the trap on this thing, Bascomb told himself. It was an interesting coincidence, but pure coincidence nonetheless—a sound, statistically understandable causation would be forthcoming in due time.

With that comforting thought, Bascomb completed the remainder of the trip and reached home.

SARAH WAS waiting anxiously, her supper schedule upset by the uncertainty of his time of arrival. She demanded at once: "Tell me all about it, Charles."

He'd thought he'd brush over it lightly in the telling. Somehow he didn't feel like describing the exhausting details of the interviews with his wife. But within a couple of hours after supper she had it all—through proper questioning, which was one of the skills in which she excelled.

Even down to Dr. Magruder.

"You mean you went away without even asking who he was?" Sarah demanded.

"It wasn't important," said Bascomb, irritated now by the cross-examination. "Besides, she'd already slammed the door in my face."

"You should have found out about him," said Sarah thoughtfully looking across his left shoulder. "I *feel* there's something important about him. Magruder—I've heard that name somewhere. Dr. Magruder—"

She went for the paper on the other side of the living room and came back, opening it in front of them. "There!" she said. "I thought I remembered."

Bascomb stared at the four inch, two column advertisement indicated by his wife's Firehouse Red fingernail.

"Are you a living vegetable—or are you living?" it asked. *"If you are dissatisfied with life, let Dr. J. Coleman Magruder show you the way to better health, vitality, and happiness. Half-alive is no better than dead. Hear Dr. Magruder Wednesday night at 8 p.m.—"*

"I guess *that* takes care of the importance of Dr. Magruder," said Mr. Bascomb with a slight feeling of triumph.

Sarah Bascomb looked thoughtfully at the advertisement for a long time, then slowly closed the paper. "I don't think so," she said finally. "I'll bet that if you go back to everyone of those people you talked to today, you'll find they have taken Dr. Magruder's course."

"Nonsense!" Bascomb cried, more sharply than he intended. "That's ridiculous! What grounds have you got for suggesting such a coincidence?"

"It's no coincidence, darling; I'm just sure that's the way it is. What Mrs. Harpersvirg said proves it—"

"It proves no such thing! Just because one flippety female said Magruder—what the devil *did* she say? I've forgotten now, but it doesn't prove all these people fell for this quack's line!"

"Ask them," said Sarah.

HE LEFT Dr. Sherridan until last. After all the rest had confirmed Sarah's hypothesis, Bascomb fought against the final prospect. It was absurd in the extreme even to suppose that Dr. Sherridan had attended quack Magruder's lectures.

But he had to know.

Dr. Sherridan smiled amiably and waved his hand in disparagement of any significance attaching to his enrollment with Dr. Magruder. "It was mostly for laughs," he said; "you know how those things go. You work hard all day without much relief from the constant pressure, and something comes up that tickles your funnybone. You go through with it just for kicks, and find you get a whale of a lift out of it; that's the way it was with this Magruder thing."

"He's a complete phony, of course, a quack?"

"Oh, naturally, but I went along with it all. I even took his pills after I had them analyzed and found out they were genuine vitamins with a harmless filler. Pretty low on vitamins, of course."

"He *has* pills?"

"Yes. Several colors for different days of the week."

"How did you come to—ah, enroll with Magruder in the first place?"

"MY PATIENTS talked about him all the time. He came by giving his lectures and enrolled most of the females over twenty-five—he's got a good line, and a nice bedside manner—and one half the neurotic males. Big crowd. So I went down to the first one of his second series to see what went on. That's how I got in; it was rather amusing, all told."

"I see. Well, I was just curious. Wife's become interested, and I wondered if it might be something the police ought to know about. Thanks for your time."

"Not at all. You might try signing up yourself if you feel in need of a laugh."

Before he went back to Landbridge, Bascomb made a check. He didn't want to have Sarah suggesting it first. And he was right: Dr. Magruder had also been to Topworth and Burraston and all of the four other cities showing insurance claims anomalies.

HE CONFESSED this additional information as soon as he got in the house that evening, in order to forestall Sarah. He should have known better than to try.

"Oh, I could have told you last night that I felt Magruder had been to all those towns; but I knew you'd say it was silly. Anyway, I'm glad you found out. I made reservations for both of us for his full course, starting tonight. We'll have to hurry to get through dinner and everything before we leave."

He tried to assess his feelings as he stood before the mirror later in their bedroom, trying to adjust his tie. Only two days ago, Hadley had shown him an innocent problem concerning claims anomalies. Tonight, as a direct result, he was signed up for a quack health and development course. A kind of fogginess seemed to develop in his mind when Bascomb tried to trace the intervening steps of this cause and effect relationship. It made no sense whatever.

He wasn't quite sure why he didn't put his foot down— even now—and declare the whole thing ridiculous, as it actually was, and refuse to go. It felt almost as if he'd been drawn into a swiftly moving current from which he didn't have the stamina to withdraw. But that was ridiculous, too; there was nothing about the whole affair that wasn't.

Except the cold, unavoidable fact that people by the dozen had bought New England policies and made claims a month or two later.

Charles Bascomb had a sense of cold foreboding as he looked at himself in the mirror now.

CHAPTER THREE

THE DOCTOR had rented the most plush assembly room in the town's best hotel, and it was filled to the limits of the gray velvet drapes upon its walls. They wouldn't have had a seat at all if Sarah hadn't insisted they hurry.

Charles Bascomb glanced about as he sat down, assessing the crowd who had turned out to hear Magruder. They were easily typed: Ninety percent of them were heavily loaded with psychosomatic ills that had already blossomed into heart trouble, cancer, arthritis, and diabetes in two thirds of them. This year they were here to listen to Magruder. Last year it had been Hongi, or something like that, from India; the year before, the sour cream and road tar molasses man; next year somebody else. Always the same crowd, minus the ones who died in between, augmented by the gullible newcomers—

Bascomb felt sorry for them; he wished he could have taken them to his office and shown them his statistics. There was the record of what would happen to this group and all the Magruders, Hongis, and sour cream men in creation couldn't change it.

Why was *he* here—when he had claims anomalies to analyze!

A solid round of applause indicated that the performance was about to begin. Somebody had stepped to the platform and was holding a hand up for attention. Bascomb thought this was Magruder, at first—but it turned out to be only the proprietor of the local health food store, who was sponsoring the course and was about to introduce his star.

He took quite a while, but Magruder finally came onstage. This was a shock. Bascomb had been expecting a barrel-chested, big-biceped character of the kind usually photographed in high society surroundings, with his arms carelessly about the waists of a couple of movie star devotees.

Instead, Dr. Magruder was a rather wizened, pinched-up little man of better than fifty. He peered myopically at his audience through broad lenses and began speaking in scratchy tones that grated on the ears.

Bascomb sat up at attention. This was decidedly different from the show he'd expected. Something was definitely not right about Magruder; he just wasn't the type of character to be putting on a show of this kind. Bascomb decided to listen.

HE WOULD have been better off if he hadn't, he decided at the end of an hour. With the aid of an incredible pseudo-biochemistry, and large charts that bore no resemblance to any structure in the human body, Dr. Magruder gave out the usual line. He spoke of "corporeal vibrations", the "ethereal stream", the "pre-science aura", and a dozen other coined phrases of nonsense. He spoke of the "correlating affinities" which his little colored pills were guaranteed to organize within the body, and of the "cosmic mono-regression" which his set of seventy-five special mental and physical exercises was sure to nullify.

It was sheer gibberish, and the audience ate it up.

Including Sarah.

She beamed happily as she received their copies of the first six of the fabulous exercises and a week's rainbow assortment of pills.

"You aren't going to *take* those things, I hope!" Bascomb whispered.

"Of course I am; and so are you. Don't you think it's wonderful that the Doctor has discovered all these things about human beings, that people have been trying to find out for so long?"

"Look, darling—"

"Don't you just *feel* the power in what Dr. Magruder says? Don't you just *know* he's right?"

Bascomb gave up and carried the exercise books and boxes of colored pills to the car, as they broke away from the crowd leaving the assembly room.

Following Sarah's admonition, he took a red and a green pill before going to bed.

THESE claims anomalies did not constitute the first items of interest, which young Hadley had brought to Bascomb's attention. Because he hoped to rise high and fast in the firm, Hadley had made an exhaustive study of his associates and superiors. It would have surprised Bascomb to know how full the file was which Hadley kept securely hidden at home, and which described the Bascomb eccentricities and foibles as Hadley saw them.

So in accord with the policy he'd adopted toward Bascomb, Hadley approached the following morning about ten o'clock—when the morning rush of mail was out of the way—with a news clipping in his hand. "Something curious here," he said. "I wondered if you might have seen it in the paper this morning."

He laid it on the desk and Bascomb frowned at it wordlessly. His cold reception of it gave Hadley a start of fear that he might have misjudged Bascomb's interest in the anomalous, after all.

"At least we can't blame Magruder for that, anyway," Bascomb growled unpleasantly.

"Who, sir?" said Brooks politely.

"Magruder. Oh, hell—I'd forgotten you didn't know anything about *him*. Forget it. Thanks for the clipping."

He turned away to his work, but Hadley stood hesitantly by the desk still. "Did you—were you able to make anything out of the claims anomalies I mentioned the other day?"

"No, nothing," Bascomb snapped irritably. Hadley fled.

BASCOMB forgot the clipping until he turned back to that side of the desk again fifteen minutes later; his eyes caught it and he read it through once more.

There was a four-inch item about a small town in Minnesota that had finally determined what to do about the TV menace to its children and its culture. On a bright spring Saturday afternoon the citizens had carried their sets down to the Town Square. There, amid picnic surroundings of fried chicken and peach cobbler, they'd had contests of sorts for various ages—the contests consisting of hurling rocks through twenty-one inch picture tubes from various distances.

Then they'd piled all the sets together and set fire to them. It was reported that there had subsequently been a run on the local library, and that discussion forums and chamber music groups had sprung up all over town.

Bascomb grinned wryly to himself. That was taking the bull—literally!—by the horns and tossing it. He hoped it indicated a trend.

But his statistician's mind veered back to the essential element in the story, the one which had prompted Hadley to cut it out: the anomaly. When umpteen hundreds of thousands of other communities throughout the land darkened their living rooms at sunset to bask in the hypnotic glow of buncombe until bedtime; why had the single town of Myersville reared up on its hind legs and demonstrated independence of national mores?

Bascomb didn't know, and he was quite sure he would never find out. His hands too full of Dr. Magruder even to think of tracking down such a remote incident as that in Myersville. But, he repeated fervently to himself, he hoped it was indicative of a trend.

He had reached a standstill in his attempts to analyze the insurance claim anomalies scientifically, according to the principles of statistics; he had to have more data. And while it seemed ridiculous to wait upon Dr. Magruder for that, yet Bascomb had just about decided there was nothing else to do.

He knew there could be no connection, but there seemed nowhere else to look for data.

HE KNOCKED off a little early for lunch. He had an appointment with an old college friend, Mark Sloane, who had suggested for weeks that they get together when he was in town. He phoned during the morning to announce this was the day.

Bascomb had been close friends with Sloane at one time, and it was nice to see him again—although Sloane had gone into advertising and was now president of his own up and coming firm. That meant they talked of advertising when they got together for lunch.

Sloane greeted Bascomb affably, but there was something lacking, which Bascomb detected at once. They selected a table and Bascomb eyed his friend critically while the menu was being brought.

"You look as if you had a rough trip this time," he said.

"If you only knew!" Sloane fanned the air in mock desperation. "I'm going to tell you about it—maybe you can help me, too. Seems like a statistician could diagnose the corpse better than anyone else, at that."

He launched into his troubles after their orders were brought. "We spent two solid months building up this campaign," he said; "we'd planned to try it in a half dozen Pacific Coast towns and then spread it nationally. We put everything we had into it—all we'd learned in fifteen years of pushing breakfast cereals and cement blocks. And it busted, went completely flat. People walked past the stacks of Singing Suds in the supermarkets as if they'd never heard the name.

"It's all over the trade. In America, *anybody* can sell soap, but Sloane and Franklin couldn't push Singing Suds. Unless we do something quick to show it isn't a habit, the soap company isn't the only one who'll go on the rocks.

"It's got us scared, Charles; I don't mind admitting it. We did everything just right, and it was a bust. Do you think you could do anything to help us find out why?"

BASCOMB leaned back thoughtfully. He had never sympathized particularly with Sloane's endeavors, but he understood what it meant to a man to take a heavy business setback like this.

"I can't do it personally, Mark, but I think somebody in my field could probably do you some good. There are several good men on the West Coast; I'll give you the names of two or three if you like."

"I wish you would," said Sloane morosely. "The worst part of it is not merely people's ignoring our campaign completely, but the fact that they bought wholesale lots of a completely unknown product called Dud's Suds. We tried to figure if the name had anything to do with it, but we couldn't pin it down.

"Dud's Suds, we found out, is put up locally and hasn't spent a nickel for advertising in years. It used to be in the little corner groceries; within the past few weeks, has pushed into the supermarkets—past nice packages like Singing Suds— It's put up in a repulsive blue, cubical box that any package man would tell you wouldn't sell in a million years. That's what has us more scared than anything else—the fact that we couldn't buck poor competition like that. We must have done something terribly wrong!"

"Call these men," Bascomb suggested, passing over a slip of paper with a couple of names and addresses on it. "They both have small polling organizations, as well as statistical services. Let them give it a try.

"There's one thing I've been wondering about since you first mentioned this: which is the better of the two soaps— Singing Suds or Dud's Suds?"

Sloane moved his hands disparagingly. "The other people's soap is better—but what's that got to do with it?"

THERE HAD been other times in his life when Charles Bascomb felt this way, and he didn't like it at all. It was a vague, indefinable feeling that things were snowballing on him and he was powerless to do anything about it.

The worst part was in not knowing just *what* was snowballing. He had freely in mind the irritations of the past few days: the short policy claims; the gnawing little newsclipping Hadley showed him, the story of Sloane's ad campaign that had bungled. But there was something *beyond* these things—yet somehow connected with each one of them—and he didn't know what it was. From a national standpoint, there was no possible connection between these events; yet something nagging faintly in his mind suggested there was.

He grew snappier around the office, and Sarah read the signs and kept quiet around the house. She knew something was bothering Charles, and it was something *big*.

In this mood he went with Sarah to the second of Dr. Magruder's lectures on Saturday night. More intently than before, he listened to the quack doctor. And more than ever he was convinced that there was something basically wrong in the show Magruder was putting on. The nub of it was that Magruder just didn't have what it took to be this kind of spieler. At his age, if he'd been in the racket a long time, he'd have had a smooth flowing delivery and a patter that would sell corn plasters to a fish.

Instead, Magruder clomped along—almost painfully at times—in his rasping voice. He paused frequently, as if uncertain just how to proceed with the group before him. He was not at all at home in what he was doing. He acted more like a ready-to-be-retired college professor.

College professor.

A small trickle of cold started on the back of Bascomb's neck and moved slowly up to the base of his skull. There was no doubt about it. There was only one place Magruder could have learned a delivery like that: on a college lecture platform.

He sat back during the rest of the discourse, alternately congratulating himself on his astuteness in seeing through Magruder's deception and berating himself for being so impulsive. No self-respecting professor would ever stoop to such jargon.

AT THE END of the period, there was a question and answer session. Well dressed matrons held up their hands without a qualm and asked items like: "If one's corporeal vibrations are out of phase with the ethereal stream, can they be brought back merely through use of exercise Four—or must the medication be relied on also to accomplish this effect?"

Magruder seemed pleased, as if the ladies were really getting his message.

Then, after a dozen of these, Bascomb stood up. "I'd like to ask," he said slowly, "how the reorganization of one's corporeal vibrations affects his need of life insurance—or of another kind, for that matter."

There was a small titter from somewhere behind him, as if such prosaic matters were beneath consideration in the same breath with corporeal vibrations. But from Magruder there was a sudden, dead stillness. Then he removed his spectacles, wiped them carefully, and peered down at Bascomb as if wanting to fix him indelibly in mind.

"Your question is a little advanced for our present discussion," Magruder finally answered in precise tones; "but for your information I may say that insurance is an excellent form of purchase when one has need of it. Otherwise, it is a waste of funds."

Bascomb nodded profoundly in agreement. "Yes, I would say that it is," he said. "I have another question: would you say that one with properly phased corporeal vibrations would be likely to spend much time watching television?"

Again Magruder did a faint double-take and peered at Bascomb. "Your question is almost irrelevant," he said, "but not entirely. As with most instruments of mass communication, television finds man in the astonishing position of having vast resources for exchange of intelligence—but no intelligence to exchange. Until this situation is corrected I would say the answer to your inquiry is no."

"One more," said Bascomb.

"Would you say that such a person would be unyielding to the ordinary advertising appeal?"

"The same answer as to your previous question," said Magruder, "and for essentially the same reason. Now, if we may continue—"

ON MONDAY, without telling anyone—including Sarah—of his intentions, Bascomb hired a firm of private investigators. Within twenty-four hours he had the information he sought. Magruder was indeed a fake; he was actually Emeritus Professor Magruder of Bay City College, a small institution in southern California. He had been head of the psychology department there and had retired two years ago at the age of sixty-five.

Bascomb took the information over the phone and promised to send a check to the investigating firm for their services. He hung up, without being aware of having done so, and continued to stare at the facts he had written down. A nightmare parade seemed to be assembling in the far depths of his mind and was already beginning its march along the channels of his cortex.

"Both John and I felt this was the time to take out a policy—you never know when you might need it."

But *they* knew!

"There's something in this that could mean a greet deal to our future, Charles." That was Sarah. Did she have any inkling of *how* much it could mean?

"It was reported that Donny Tompkins won the twelve year olds' slingshot event by putting a rock through a twenty-one inch screen from a distance of one hundred and ten yards."

"It has us scared, Charles. The other people's soap is better, but what has that got to do with it?"

How many more? How many more— In a country as big as the United States? He'd only come across a whisper of the anomaly. What would he find if he really looked—

He put on his hat and went out to get a taxi for Magruder's hotel.

CHAPTER FOUR

THE PROFESSOR greeted Charles Bascomb at the door with an extended hand. With the other he dropped a cigarette into an overflowing ashtray. "I'm glad you finally came," Magruder said. "I waited all day yesterday for you; I had begun to fear I was anticipating too much."

"It took me that long to run down the dope on you," said Bascomb. He passed into the moderately untidy room with its thick cloud of stale smoke. He opened a window and looked out.

Finally, he turned. "I know who you are, but that's about all. I know you are doing something to the business of my insurance company, but I don't know how. You weren't surprised by my questions about television and advertising, so I must assume you know what I was referring to. I get cold along the back of my neck and down my spine when I think of what I don't know about you.

"I don't believe any of it, of course; it's too fantastic to believe. But here I am. And you were waiting for me. Now it's your turn to talk, Professor."

Magruder smiled and settled back in a chair opposite Bascomb. "You are a blunt man, for a statistician," he said. "I find the uncertainties of their profession ordinarily extends to their common speech."

Bascomb eyed him without answering. Magruder seemed to be musing now on something seen through the windows—but this was the tenth floor, and there was only sky beyond.

He didn't change the focus of his eyes as he said, "Insurance is actually a most reprehensible business, isn't it, Mr. Bascomb?"

Bascomb decided against rising to the bait.

"Making money from people's certainty of death or misfortune—a ghoulish business. But then, since your own profession assists this traffic in misery, I suppose it is difficult for you to see it. May I ask, Mr. Bascomb, how many of the capsules you have taken and how many hours of the exercises you have performed?"

BASCOMB stirred with vigor for the first time. "That nonsense! Come on, Professor, let's have the genuine story of what you are trying to do. I'm not one of those fat old matrons in your audiences, remember."

"But that *is* the genuine story," said Magruder. "Because I have somewhat disguised it with a bit of mummery, do you suppose the whole thing is trickery?"

"That's what I'm trying to find out. Everything I've heard so far in your lectures is nonsense—and of course the feeble vitamin pills you dish out are of no importance."

"And that is where you are wrong," said Magruder. "I must ask you to answer my question if you will, please."

"Oh, I've been taking your damned pills!" Bascomb answered irritably. "I have to, to keep peace in the house; you've got my wife thoroughly buffaloed with your double talk. I've been doing the exercises, too. She insists on it every evening."

"Good. Then perhaps you can understand something of what I have to say—although it may be a trifle early for full comprehension.

"Can you imagine what it would be like to live in a world, Mr. Bascomb, where insurance companies were not needed?"

"Certainly not; it's ridiculous to even contemplate. Insurance business provides a sound, social need in spreading the risks of modern living. To destroy the insurance business would once again make the individual the prey of all the unforeseen and uncontrollable forces of nature and our complex civilization, from which he is now protected."

Magruder looked out the window again, as if he had almost forgotten his visitor. Then he said at last, "Doesn't it seem curious to you that modern man, with all his tremendous technological accomplishments, should still be in such great need of protection from these forces?"

"No," said Bascomb; "biology teaches us that man was forced to develop auxiliary protections because of his inherent physical weakness. That's what's made him great; out of weakness has come his strength."

"AND WHAT basis is there for such a preposterous assumption?" Magruder showed angry excitement for the first time. "How could Man have reached the top of the evolutionary ladder if he dropped his natural, physical protective devices, one by one, as he developed? Can you think of a hypothesis more absurd than this one? Wouldn't he, rather, have accumulated survival instruments instead of dropping them?"

"He did," said Bascomb. "His brain—which enables him to devise any means of protection and development that he needs."

"And that's an improvement, I suppose! A device to manufacture out of crude metal and glass the instruments possessed for fifty to a hundred million years by other species. The swift knows with unerring accuracy the way to go to avoid an oncoming storm, and its temporarily-abandoned young go into hibernation when it comes. But human beings still don't know which way to duck a hurricane; and the ones caught in it die.

"For fifty million years bats have navigated by sonar. An eel-like fish of the Nile uses true electromagnetic radar. But Man is just now getting around to clumsy mechanical duplicates of these devices. Birds and animals use the polarization of daylight to determine direction and time. Man still hasn't got a really practical device for duplicating this feat.

"The homing ability of the 'lower species' is traditional. We use 'bird-brain' as a term of insult—but it takes quite a few tons of iron and glass even to approach a duplication of the functions of a two or three ounce bird brain."

"Are you suggesting, then," said Bascomb with a superior smile, "that Man should take a backward step and pick up some of the abilities of his distant forebears?"

"Is it anything to boast of that Man lacks the abilities of the lower species?" Magruder snapped. "Actually, they're not lost; Man doesn't have to go back. What I'm suggesting is that he merely bring into full play those abilities he has—for he does indeed stand at the top of the evolutionary ladder!

"Man's homing ability is superior to that of the pigeon, or of the elephant, fish, or bat—which have it in abundance. His natural radar sense excels that of the Nile fish; his sonar is better than that found in bats and rats. And his prescience of disaster far outdistances that of the swift."

"You mean we have all these mechanisms, unused, within the structure of our bodies?"

Magruder shook his head. "No. The mechanisms we see in the lower species are clumsy experimental models. In Man, Nature has installed the final production model, which incorporates all the prior successes without their bugs, as I believe an engineer would say it.

"This final production model we call 'intuition'."

BASCOMB choked; for a moment he felt like laughing out loud. He had a flashing vision of Sarah before him— arms akimbo and lips pressed tightly while she exclaimed, "I don't care what you say, Charles Bascomb, I *know* what's right, and that's the way it's going to be done!"

It made no difference what *'it'* was. Sarah's feeling of just knowing could be applied to anything.

And then Bascomb had a mental picture, too, of Mrs. Davidson and Mrs. Harpersvirg and Dr. Sherridan.

He permitted only a faint smile as he finally answered.

"You believe you have tamed man's ability to do things by hunch and guesswork?"

"Unreasonable, isn't it?" said Magruder. "It helps just a little if you use the proper terminology, however. Intuition is a definite, precise faculty of the human organism; evolution-wise, it stands at the peak of all those faculties we have been talking about in the lower species. It supplants them all, and goes beyond anything they can accomplish. And human beings have it. All of them."

"That's a large order of unsubstantiated statements."

Magruder's eyebrows lifted. "I thought I'd given you some rather remarkable evidence in your own field. You want more? Very well, I'll give you the names of an even dozen people in Wallsenburg where I finished a series of lectures last month. They will buy policies—not necessarily with your company—and will make claims within a month. You'll find them, if you check; can I give you any more evidence?"

BASCOMB shifted uncomfortably. "Let's say for the moment that I accept your thesis. Why, then, has intuition— particularly among the female of the species—become a stock joke? Why have men, generally, never been able to rely on the intuition they're supposed to have? How are you able to do anything about making it usable? Surely, these colored pills, and the nonsense you lecture about—"

"Did you ever watch a person read with his lips moving, forming every word?" said Magruder. "Irritating as the devil, isn't it? You want to tell him to quit flapping his chops—that he can read ten times as fast if he'll go about it right.

"Men don't always choose to use the maximum ability that is in them; the answer to your question is as simple as that. Men decided a long time ago not to use intuitive powers, and employ something else."

"What else?" asked Bascomb.

"Statistics," said Magruder.

Bascomb felt a warm anger rising within him. That was the kind of thing you could expect, he supposed, from a broken down professor turned quack. He forgot his recent interviews for a moment.

"I fail to see any need for an attack on the principles of statistics," he said. "Statistics enable predictions to be made, which would be impossible otherwise."

"Predictions about a *group*," said Magruder; "not individuals. Consider your own business. Statistical laws enable the insurance company to function, and make a profit for its shareholders. But what does statistics do for the policyholder? *Not one damn thing!*

"Think it over; you're not working for the policyholder. He's absolutely defenseless against whatever assessment your statistics tell you is legitimate to levy against him. The individual gets absolutely nothing from your work. The group—the shareholders of the company—are the only ones who benefit."

"I'VE NEVER heard anything quite so ridiculous in my whole life!" said Bascomb heatedly.

"No?" Magruder smiled softly. "Let's consider the alternative situation then—one in which the policyholder is on an even-Stephen basis, so to speak, with the company.

"Suppose he is able to discern—as a number of people you've met recently can do—the precise need for insurance which may come his way. He doesn't need to pay premiums uselessly for twenty or thirty years, and get nothing for them; but when he sees an unavoidable emergency approaching a month or so away, he can take out a policy to cover it. There's something he can really benefit from!"

"Quite obviously, you don't understand the principles of the insurance business at all," said Bascomb. "It would simply cease to exist if what you described were a widespread possibility."

"Ah, yes," sighed Magruder, "that is quite true. Insurance would become obsolete as an institution, and would be replaced by common sense planning on the part of the individual. Any remnant of the insurance concept would have to be strictly on a loan basis.

"The same fate will be true for numerous other institutions that operate for the group at the expense of the individual—our concept of education, the jury system and criminal punishment. The advertising business as we know it will disappear; mass media of communication will operate only during the infrequent intervals, when there's something to communicate—"

"You speak as if you considered the Group as some all-powerful enemy the individual must combat for his own survival!"

"To a large extent that is true."

"To a greater extent it's absolute nonsense, and the psychiatrists have a word for it."

"Yes," Magruder agreed. "They have a word for nearly every thing—I wonder what they will call your bankrupt insurance company."

"I don't consider that my company is in any danger whatever. I am quite certain that, while your hypotheses are very entertaining, I can eventually find a sound statistical explanation for this sudden run of claims on short time policies."

"And for my prediction of an additional dozen?" Magruder spread his hands inquiringly.

BASCOMB didn't answer. Instead he asked, "Why were you expecting me to come to see you? Why did you *want* me to come?"

"Because I need the understanding of men like you. I need men who know what it's like to be on both sides of the statistical fence, so to speak. I thought you were capable of becoming one."

"I'm sorry you were wrong, and have had to waste much valuable time," said Bascomb. "I must admit that I have a great curiosity about your insistent attack on statistics. You've made no case against it; and certainly it operates well enough—in a society of us non-intuitionists, at least."

"Which is the only place it will work," said Magruder. "Admittedly, this concept of intuition is so foreign to our present thinking that it appears to be an approach to insanity. We are so accustomed in our culture to the dominance of Society over Individual that we are unable to realize it as unnecessary.

"No historical era can match today's demand by the Individual for security and assurance from sources outside himself; no era can match this one for such complete overshadowing of the Individual by Society, the Nation, the Empire—not even ancient times when slavery was an acceptable culture. The slaves would revolt on occasion; the Individual does not revolt today."

"And so you envision the ultimate anarchy!" Bascomb exclaimed in astonishment. "The wild lawlessness of the individual supreme, unimpeded by the restrictions of government?"

"I HAVE said no such thing," Magruder said angrily. "Man's optimum functioning demands his membership in a group. It's impossible for him to go it alone—on a cultural level, at least. But neither can he function optimally until he invents a society that does not oppress him to its own supposed advantage—until one man's worth is adequately balanced against that of the entire Society."

"So our Society is the enemy to be fought then?" Bascomb thought he had Magruder's number now, and he was ready to laugh. Being taken in by a mere subversive!

"No." Magruder smiled now as if reading Bascomb's thoughts. "No—Man is his own enemy—by mis-arrangement. He invented Society, and didn't know he could do so much better; it is up to him to correct his own error."

Bascomb felt a little wave of cold. He spoke with increased care. "So your objective is to destroy Society? That's a trifle ambitious, to say the least. There've been a good many attempts to do that same thing in the past, but it manages to struggle along."

"Shocking thought, is it not?" said Magruder. "Well, fortunately, it's a misconception. My objective is not, of course, to destroy Society, as such, but rather to permit the emergence of a kind of man who will no longer have use for what we call Society.

"PLEASE understand, there's nothing sacred whatever in the word or the thing we call Society. It's an invention of mankind—who has as much right to change, repair, or substitute for it as he has with any of his other inventions. First, there was Man: Society came later. Let's go back and consider the time when there was only Man.

"He was an infant, just learning to read, if you will. And the job was tough, because it required that he be self-taught. He didn't learn the best way; he learned to read by moving his lips, and he never tried seriously to improve upon this.

"To drop the analogy now for the real circumstances: Man found there were numerous ways of solving problems and reaching generalizations about the world around him. He could get his own answer on an individual basis and go ahead and apply it, for one way. But he'd already learned that, on a strictly physical level, there was strength in numbers; so he was suspicious of the solitary approach to anything. He developed the method of comparing proposed solutions to problems with his fellows. Sometimes there was a radical difference—the same problem affected different Individuals in widely varying ways. But it seemed like a good idea to stick together instead of going it alone. Compromises were made; the consensus of opinion was taken, and the majority decision accepted by all.

"Thus was born Society—and with it the art of statistics, the submergence of the Individual in the Group."

"I don't know where you learned your sociology, Professor—but if anything like the scene you describe actually occurred, that was the birth of Man's triumph over a nature he could not combat single-handed. It was the birth of his realization that the combined effort of many individuals can accomplish what none of them can do alone."

"No," said Magruder. "This is not what was born at that time. A concerted attack on Man's problems does not depend on his present Society. Cooperation is more easily obtained through much different instruments.

"WITHOUT exerting himself to work out such different instruments, however, Man was forced to cling desperately to the tool of his invention, Society. Inherent within it was the concept that the Individual was a servant of the group. In any question of conflicting welfare the Individual expected automatic defeat; sometimes he has fought against it, but never with any heart or expectancy of winning.

"Statistical methods were the obvious intellectual tools with which to manipulate and describe Man as he functioned in Society. The Individual was of no import, so why bother devising a means of accommodating him? In writing insurance policies, it is important to you to know only that one out of a certain dozen men will die of cancer. *Which* one is of no concern to you—unless it is yourself or someone for whom you have an affection. In this case, however, you have lost your usefulness to Society as an impartial statistician, and Society will replace you.

"As a method of reasoning, which would fit his Society, Man developed logic-statistical induction of generalizations from many individual instances. It works fine in predicting the characteristics of the group, but no individual instance can be deduced from it.

"But from time to time there have appeared short bursts of a stronger, more subtle, and completely incomprehensible means of reaching a generalization—the one Man by-passed when he invented Society; the non-logical process called intuition.

"Within the framework of our culture it has been impossible to describe, and the conclusions reached could not be defended in any logical manner acceptable to Society."

BASCOMB shifted uneasily. "And now you have corrected these defects?" he said.

"Yes," said Magruder. "Men can now be taught how to reach generalizations through the method of intuition. And please note that the inductive operation by the intuitive method yields a different type of generalization. The intuitive generalization is of the type of the Natural Law, which, unlike the Statistical Generalization, does permit deduction of individual instances.

"The intuitive method, therefore, is the only one that does an individual any good!"

"And you can no doubt *prove* as well as teach what you say," said Bascomb.

Magruder smiled. "The proof, as well as the method, is one which Society is loath to accept. The pragmatic test—in itself a non-logical method—is the only one applicable. I think, however, it has been applied sufficiently to allow you to reach a conclusion!"

"A man would have to possess a very large dose of sheer faith in order to live by intuition if he could never prove a hypothesis until it had been tried in actual experience."

"Yes," Magruder nodded soberly. "I would say that faith is a large component of intuition."

"There is only one thing you have left out: the mechanism by which these weird exercises of body and mind, and the little colored pills are supposed to restore one's intuition."

"That, too," said Magruder, "is something that can only be tested pragmatically. You understand, of course, that these methods do not restore anything. *You* have never learned to use intuition in any degree; your wife is considerably more proficient. Yet, comparatively speaking, you are both readers who move your lips. You have to learn to do it by scanning—and the only proof that this is better is in learning it.

"SO, IF YOU continue, you will learn how to use your intuitive powers. The little pills contain a shading of vitamins to satisfy those curious enough to analyze them. The active ingredient is the other material, which is necessary to subdue the automatic reaction of fear in dropping statistical thinking. This fear is very real and dominating; it says that use of intuition is a defiance of the billions of a man's fellows who have lived since the beginning of the race. It says they will crush him for daring to step out on his own and be an Individual who does not consult and bow to their wishes.

"Without a proper biochemical compensation of this fear, it would be all but impossible for a man to ever command his intuitive powers. So do not attempt it without use of the pills; it would tear you to pieces."

"And one final question," said Bascomb. "If I were to believe all this, and become one of your men who 'know what it's like to be on both sides of the statistical fence,' what use would you make of me?"

"I would ask you to assist in the spread of these methods, particularly among your own professional group, which is among the strongest fortresses that intuition has to attack. Such attack can best be done by someone from the inside."

"I see." Bascomb rose suddenly and took up his hat. "It has been most entertaining, Professor; many thanks for your time."

"Not at all." Magruder smiled and accompanied him to the door. "I will expect you at the next lecture."

"It is doubtful I will be there," said Bascomb. "Quite doubtful."

CHAPTER FIVE

BASCOMB had it in mind to return to the office as he left Magruder's hotel room, but once out on the street he knew this was impossible. His brain churned with the impossible mixture of fantasy and faintly credible truth, which Magruder had dispensed.

He turned down the street in the direction away from his up-town office and moved slowly, dimly aware of his surroundings, murmuring apologies to his fellow pedestrians with whom he collided at intervals. Finally, he stopped and found an empty bench in Moller's Park; he sat down, the pigeons clustering expectantly about his feet.

He had nothing to feed them, but their random motion and the sharp whine of their wings served to bring him in closer touch with the present moment.

A decision had to be made and made quickly. There was no use quibbling mentally over what Magruder could or could not do. The critical fact was that he could do *something*. Charles Bascomb had no doubt of this; he simply could not deny the run of policy claims. How much of all that nonsense about intuition was true Bascomb didn't know; for the moment he didn't care. Magruder was far more than a harmless quack; he was a crank—and a dangerous one at that. If his mysterious doings were extended any further, he could actually undermine the foundations of the nation's insurance business.

He *could*.

And how much more beyond that, Bascomb didn't know; there would be time enough to find out when Magruder was safely stopped.

He considered going to the police with his story, but almost at once the futility of this was obvious. What desk sergeant, detective, or even police chief would listen to such a tale without being tempted to throw *him* behind bars for drunkenness?

Magruder had rightly said the only test of his theories and work was the pragmatic one. And until a person had seen actual results he would be convinced the whole thing was the product of an active insanity.

There had to be a more indirect method.

AT ONCE, Bascomb thought of his friend, Hap Johnson, feature writer of the *Courier;* Hap would understand a thing like this. He would take the obvious view, at first, that Bascomb was drunk; but his innate curiosity wouldn't let him stop there. Hap was a solid citizen and a respected newspaperman; but he had just enough yen to be the kind of news hero pictured in the movies to be hooked by something like this. Yes, Hap was the man to see, Bascomb decided as he got up from the park bench.

He found his man slapping a typewriter in a small cubicle located just off the *Courier* city room. The room was full of smoke, the typewriter was very old, and Hap's hat clung to the back of his head at a sharp angle. These were the affectations he allowed himself in deference to the movie idols he realized that no workaday reporter could ever hope to emulate. Otherwise, he was an excellent newsman.

He looked up as Bascomb walked in. "Charley! Don't do a thing like that! The roof braces of this firetrap can't take such a shock. Don't tell me now—you've lost your job; your wife has left you; you owe the company ten thousand dollars you've embezzled—"

Bascomb sat down, pushing Hap back into the chair from which he'd risen. "It's worse," he said. "I want you to do me a favor—and give me some advice."

"The advice is easy," said Hap; "I don't know about the other part."

SKETCHILY, then—without going into Magruder's complex social theories—Bascomb described the professor as a half-baked quack who could really do some of the things he claimed.

"Call it hypnosis, suggestion, or whatever you want to," he said. "Magruder exerts some kind of controlling influence over the people who take his courses. Personally, I think it works through the pills he gives out. Whatever it is, the man is dangerous; he's radical, subversive and he is somehow able to lead his followers to accomplish what he wants them to do.

"Right now, he seems to be attacking the insurance companies with an eye to bankrupting them. You'll say I'm crazy, but I'm genuinely afraid of what he might be able to do if he was able to expand and make a concentrated attack. You can imagine what the results would be if he actually succeeded—financial chaos. He seems to think he can do the same kind of trick with the advertising business and other institutions. He's got to be stopped."

Hap Johnson pushed his hat a notch further back on his head and regarded Bascomb thoughtfully. "You're not a drinking man," he said, "and I've never detected signs of insanity before. So it's possible there's something in what you say. But—" he leaned closer in a gesture of secret confidence, "isn't it reasonable to suppose you might have been mistaken about the people you interviewed? Overwork, worry about the guy who's gigging for your job—"

"I'm *sure*, Hap," said Bascomb. "I've gone over it a hundred times; I've plugged every hole."

Hap drew back. "It's not the kind of thing you could go to the police with—yet they ought to know about it. Here's what we can do: you say Magruder is no M. D., so we ought to be able to get him investigated for prescribing those pills of his—practicing medicine without a license."

"I don't know whether that would stop him or not—"

"It might not *stop* him, but it would get him some darned unfavorable publicity, if it's handled right. We could play it from there. I'll get a ticket to his lecture; you can introduce me, and we'll see what kind of story he gives me."

BASCOMB neglected to tell Sarah anything about his visits with Dr. Magruder and Hap Johnson; but he caught her eyeing him as if she knew all about it, anyway. It gave him the old, familiar, uneasy sensation. He knew she couldn't possibly have learned what he'd done, but she had feelings about things; he wished he dared ask precisely what those feelings were.

On the evening of the next lecture she volunteered the information. Bascomb had just told her about arranging for Hap to go with them.

"That's what I've been feeling!" Sarah exclaimed. "It's been as if tonight were a turning point of some kind. I can't tell whether it's going to be good or bad for us—but it

depends on something that's going to happen to Dr. Magruder. And Hap Johnson is responsible! He doesn't want to come to find out what Dr. Magruder teaches; he just wants gossip for that cheap tabloid he works for, and he doesn't care who he hurts in getting it."

"I thought you liked Hap."

"I used to—until he did this to Magruder!"

"He hasn't done *anything* yet," Bascomb reminded her; "so far there's nothing but your own slightly overworking imagination."

Sarah ignored his remark. "Let's not go tonight, Charles. Don't take Hap down there; he'll kill Magruder with what he'll print."

Bascomb felt the perspiration starting under his collar. "Don't be ridiculous, darling; you're imagining things. I've asked Hap along, and he'd think I was crazy if I tried to back out now. Nothing's going to happen; you'll see."

THE EVENING seemed to go smoothly enough in spite of Bascomb's mixed anxieties. He let his attention be held only mildly by Magruder's double-talk, and afterwards, when he went up to introduce Hap Johnson the Professor smiled knowingly. Magruder's face clouded a trifle, however, as he took the reporter's hand, and Bascomb saw a new tension come at the same moment into his wife's expression.

Then it was past and Magruder was shaking Hap Johnson's hand cordially, inviting him back, making an offering of a generous sample of his pills and the circulars describing his exercises.

"This will make me a superman, huh?" Hap asked dubiously as he accepted the articles and examined them.

"Guaranteed!" Dr. Magruder slapped him on the shoulder and laughed jovially. "It never fails when instructions are followed faithfully. Of course," he added soberly, "I realize you are not sufficiently interested to go along with me to that extent; but I trust that if you write up our little course of lectures here, you will keep in mind that we actually offer nothing at all. Anything that occurs as a result of coming here is due strictly to the student's own efforts."

"If that were true," said the reporter with sudden iciness in his eyes, "it would not be necessary for you to hold lectures at all, would it? The buck isn't passed as easily as all that!"

ON THE way home, Bascomb tried to console his wife; he reminded her repeatedly that nothing had happened to verify her fears. Sarah remained unresponsive, apparently accepting as fact that Magruder's doom was sealed. She felt it, she said.

Bascomb drove carefully, acutely aware of the sense of exhaustion that filled him. It was futile to close his eyes any longer to the fact that Sarah's feelings corresponded exactly with Magruder's description of a moderately well working intuition.

In the early years of their marriage, he'd laughed at her and shrugged off her hunches and lucky guesses; then he'd begun to keep tab—

There was no question about her knowing Hap's purpose in coming to the meeting. Bascomb wondered how much she was aware of his own position. She had nothing, but her intuitive knowledge shown bleakly in her eyes, he thought miserably.

He hadn't quite known, at first, just why he felt it necessary to keep from telling her about his visit with Magruder and Hap. Now he saw the full impossibility of it. Suppose Magruder were right—well, partly right, anyway? Suppose intuition did turn out to be a natural, useful human function that was active in some people and could be developed in others? How could he tell Sarah that Magruder was an evil man—that the faculty she cherished so greatly had to be suppressed with all possible force?

She wouldn't understand that a sizeable number of intuitive people could literally destroy the civilization and institutions that modern man was dependent upon.

Her intuition was too precious a possession for Sarah to ever believe anything evil could be in it, Bascomb thought; she'd turn against him before believing that. This thing had a potential that could destroy his very home if he failed to handle it right!

In his attempts to appease her he was more than usually cooperative that night in doing the routine Magruder prescribed, and in taking the pills. They were brown and orange now.

Sarah's face did not relax its expression of foreboding.

IT OCCURRED to Bascomb, as soon as he reached the office the next morning that applications might now be coming in from the people named by Magruder in their interview. He was right; six of them were in the morning mail.

He had no actual right to enter the applications department and take a look at the papers before they had even begun to be processed. It was no great offense, of course—it wouldn't have been to a man other than the kind Dave Tremayne happened to be. Tremayne was head of the processing department. Another man's casual courtesy was his grudging favor.

Bascomb was well aware of this as he stood with the papers in his hand, scanning them while Tremayne looked on belligerently.

"These will have to be rejected," Bascomb said as mildly as possible. And for a long time afterward he wondered why he actually said it; there would be no great harm to the company in paying off claims of an additional half dozen short-term policy holders. But that thought was utterly foreign to his mind now. He could see no course but the one he was following.

"I thought that was for us to decide," Dave Tremayne snapped; "since when did the Statistical Department take over those duties?"

"I—I happen to know a little about these cases," Bascomb said hesitantly. "Friend of mine is acquainted with the town pretty well. He knows these people and is certain there is something that isn't on the level. This big fire policy for example. Bhuener's Hardware. It's a firetrap; I wouldn't be surprised if you got a claim on it before the month is out—"

Tremayne advanced and took the papers from Bascomb's hand. "You can let us worry about that," he said unpleasantly; "any time I need help from the figures department I'll let you know."

HE SHOULD have known it was worse than useless, Bascomb told himself. He looked at Tremayne and turned away; then he stopped and faced the department head again. "It wouldn't look at all good," he said, "if you got another half dozen claims within a month of granting the policies. Your short-termers are beginning to stick out on the charts."

"What do you mean by that?" Tremayne demanded. But his belligerence had subsided now.

"I'm advising you to turn down those applications," Bascomb said. He walked away to his own department.

It wasn't a logical thing to do, he thought, as he reached his own desk once again. It could cause a lot of trouble either way it fell—whether the prediction turned out right or wrong. And Dave Tremayne was just the kind to milk it for all the trouble it was worth.

He was rather hopeful of hearing something from Johnson regarding the reporter's impressions and plans concerning the campaign against Magruder. But he heard nothing at all that day, nor the next. A sense of loneliness assailed him. He wanted somebody to talk to about this thing, but there was nobody at all to give him companionship under this burden. Sarah continued moody and cool and convinced of the approach of disaster.

CHAPTER SIX

HAP JOHNSON called on the succeeding day, and he had news. "This bird is more clever than you've given him credit for!" he said. "It's no wonder the previous chemical analyses showed a harmless filler supporting a few vitamins in his pills."

"What do you mean?" said Bascomb.

"I had five different outfits run tests on these pills before I found the answer. They all gave the same story you already had. Then I asked Joe Archer, who runs toxic checks for the police department, to look at them. He got it in a minute, just by looking at the other guys' results.

"They were right. The pills are about as potent as dried carrots—individually; but put them together in the combinations and succession Magruder prescribes and you've got something—"

"What?" asked Bascomb.

"Joe couldn't give me the answer to that, but he said it was obvious these chemicals would combine in the body, and with the body chemicals, to form some items only slightly less potent than dynamite."

"We really ought to have a case against Magruder then," said Bascomb. Peculiarly, he thought, there was no sense of elation or triumph at all, now that defeat of his enemy was in sight.

"That's the devil of it," said Hap; "I'm not so sure we have. That's where Magruder has been so clever. The things he has actually been prescribing are inconsequential. I'm not so sure we could pin him down on the basis of the fact that his pills recombine inside the human system to form new and more potent drugs. He could argue he'd never prescribed or administered *those;* and, technically, he'd be right."

"But it would ruin him, even if the courts had to agree with that argument; and that's all I'm interested in," Bascomb replied. "Can't your friend, Archer, give us enough basis for a complaint to the District Attorney."

"He said it ought to be made known, at any rate. It would help if we could get some witnesses who could swear they'd been injured by the pills. Why don't you talk to Joe yourself, and see if you can round up any such witnesses? You know who's been taking in these lectures; in the meantime I'll put a gentle word in the paper to start the ball rolling."

CHARLES BASCOMB agreed and hung up. From what he'd seen, however, he doubted that it would be possible to get any of Magruder's followers to complain against him. They were a devout bunch—all those he'd seen, anyway.

A doubting weariness came over him again as he sat there staring at the black shape of the telephone. How in Heaven's name had this all begun? How had he become so involved in a senseless, unbelievable tangle like this?

Why was he the only one, out of the hundreds who'd contacted Magruder, who understood the threat of Magruder's work? It was as if the Professor had singled him out, as his greatest potential enemy, to show him exactly what he could do. And Bascomb remembered that Magruder had said this was just what he had done—in order to recruit

Bascomb's aid. But surely Magruder hadn't actually believed he'd accept the validity, and desirability of the Professor's work!

That was the dilemma presented by the whole thing. To recognize it as a threat, Magruder's claim had to be accepted as valid. A hundred times a day, Bascomb had to ask himself again if he accepted this. And because of what he had seen, his answer was still a forced, unwilling yes.

And if so incredible a work was valid, could it not function for good instead of harm? This also gnawed unceasingly in Bascomb's mind. But Magruder's own words had answered this. He was out to change the face of society in a destructive manner.

IT WASN'T just that he was selfishly thinking of the insurance business, Bascomb reminded himself; Magruder seemed bent on attacking the whole bright world of statistical science, and all the institutions founded upon it.

And this Bascomb could not countenance; his own private world had no other foundation. In statistics a man could know what to expect of the world. Destroy this, put existence on an individual incident basis, and what was left? A nebulous faith in unconfirmed beliefs about how things *ought* to turn out. Then he thought again of Sarah and felt lost.

His world had already been shaken too vigorously.

He didn't go to Joe Archer; there seemed to be no point in it yet. He continued with the pills and the exercises, and went to another lecture. There, he looked for possible witnesses against Magruder, and knew that the quest was futile, even before it started. These people *never* turned on their messiahs; even if one failed them, there was always the next season, and the next—

THAT WAS the day the first of Hap's articles appeared in the paper. He indicated he was going to do a series analyzing the weird cults and health panaceas and mental improvement fads that proved sucker traps for the sick, neurotic part of the populace, which was in need of genuine help.

It began mildly enough, as Johnson had promised; but Bascomb was more than ordinarily amazed at the man's genius, because he could see where Hap was going. He began, not by antagonizing those who were following such phony panaceas, but by sympathizing thoroughly with their search for assistance—which was so difficult to find in a brutal civilization that cared only in token measures for the sick or improvident individual.

He promised to follow up with stories of the frauds that preyed upon such people. It was a terrific build-up for the time when he was ready to let go at Magruder. Reading it, Bascomb felt the matter had already passed from his hands. Magruder was at the mercy of Hap Johnson—and the newspaper-reading public.

Bascomb felt later that he should have been prepared for the event that occurred the following day. (He was eventually to do a great deal of Monday morning quarterbacking over this period of his life.) But when he went to the office, he was still prepossessed of the thought that power to act in the Magruder matter had passed from him.

He was called almost as soon as he arrived to the office of Farnham Sprock, Second Vice-president of New England. Sprock was a small, mealy old man who had been by-passed sometime ago for the top post in the Company. He had been relegated to office administration, even though it was known that all who felt his judgment would suffer for his failure.

SPROCK looked at Bascomb through seemingly dull eyes as the statistician entered the room.

"You sent for me?" Bascomb said, trying to make it as little like a question as possible.

"I've had a most unbelievable complaint about you," said Sprock. "It seems too incredible to even act upon it, to believe that one of our Family would act in such a manner. Yet I am forced to believe that the accusation is well founded.

"I am told that you have assumed to step over the line of your authority in this office, and presume to dictate to your fellow officers in the conduct of their affairs. You have demanded that Mr. Tremayne refuse to act favorably on certain applications, so it is said. Is this true, Mr. Bascomb?"

"Yes." Bascomb nodded his head. And suddenly he felt himself shaking all over; this wizened old fool could actually destroy him if Sprock took it into his silly head. He could deny Charles Bascomb the world of facts and figures and clean, cold statistical reality. Why hadn't he minded his own business?"

"Why, Mr. Bascomb?" asked Sprock.

Bascomb took a deep breath and wearily recited the occurrence of the anomalies from beginning to end, leaving out all reference to Magruder, of course.

"All you have said is a matter of serious concern, and one we should well pay attention to," said Sprock. "But it has nothing to do with your presumption in the matter of advising Mr. Tremayne."

"I have said that the policy applications I referred to are of the same class as those previously mentioned; they will also be followed by quick claims."

Sprock rose and came around the side of his desk. "Mr. Bascomb, that is a thing you could not possibly know!"

SUDDENLY an old, latent fury seemed to spring alive inside Bascomb's mind. What was this shriveled idiot trying to tell *him*? He knew—he *knew* beyond all question of doubt that what he said was true. It didn't matter that Magruder had predicted it. Magruder had nothing to do with this positive, insistent knowledge that burned in his mind.

He knew, in and of himself, that those policies would turn out as he said. And Sprock telling him he couldn't possibly know—

As suddenly as it had arisen, the rage died, and Bascomb found himself smiling at the little man and sensing a strange pity for him.

"I have discovered something new," said Bascomb quietly. "It—it is a recent statistical development on which I have been working for some time. It is a formula that enables me to predict when we are due for a run of policies such as this. They occur every once in a while, you know; my formula tells me that this is ready to occur again."

"I don't believe it!" snapped Sprock. "Such a thing is impossible. Why if it were true, it would—it would change the entire aspect of our business. I warn you, Bascomb—and this is the last and only time I will do so—I want no repetition of this kind of occurrence. I will not tolerate it in my organization. A repetition means a complete and permanent severance of your relations with this Company. Do I make myself clear, Bascomb?"

"Yes," said Bascomb. He turned to the door as Sprock dismissed him. But he turned, with his hand on the knob. "I would suggest, however," he said, "that you get a list of those applications from Mr. Tremayne. Within thirty days there will be claims on every one of them!"

BACK AT his desk, Charles Bascomb felt a tremendous sense of release, quite unlike anything he had ever experienced before—an elation at having stood up to Sprock. He had a momentary feeling of not being afraid of Sprock any more—or of New England—or of any other force that might be able to shake him from his niche.

It died in a renewed consternation over what he'd said. Why on Earth had he invented the lie he told Sprock, the lie about a mathematical invention that would predict unfavorable runs? Well, there had to be something to cover his previous statement about knowing positively there would be claims on these particular policies.

And then the full force of what he'd said hit him. He'd said he *knew*. And it was true. He wasn't just taking Magruder's word for it, he knew. As if trapped in a corner by a persistent enemy, he tried to evade this sudden fact, to turn his back upon it and refuse to admit all its appalling implications.

But escape was impossible.

He sat there, feeling stunned, then slowly embraced the unwanted knowledge.

This was it.

This was intuition.

It was the way Sarah felt, he supposed—only she felt it on almost any connection. No wonder she thought him a blockhead when he couldn't understand how she could be so sure of a wholly illogical assumption!

It was the way the policyholders felt, too, the ones he'd interviewed. And they had been right.

IT WAS impossible to take up the thread of his work as he had planned it before receiving Sprock's call. He got up and went over to the unabridged dictionary open on its stand in the corner by the window. He turned the pages to *intuition.*

"Perceived by the mind immediately or without the intervention of any process of thought," he read. In very recent times he would have made an extremely bad pun on that definition.

"Quick perception of truth, without conscious attention or reasoning—truth obtained by internal apprehension without the aid of perception or the reasoning powers."

That last one was closest to it, he thought, but even so, it was extremely deceptive—written by a man who hadn't the faintest concept of intuition. For there could be no obtaining of truth without perception; of that Bascomb was quite sure. There had to be contact. He didn't know how he could explain his contact with the matter of the six policies, which he knew, would shortly have claims on them, but somehow there *was* contact.

He closed the book. A statistician, not an intuitionist had written the definitions, he thought wryly; and that was no help at all.

He took his hat and walked out of the office, leaving word with Miss Pilgrim, his secretary, that he'd be back after lunch.

He had no definite goal in mind. He wanted merely to get away, to try to get some self-evaluation of the thing that had happened. He half expected the experience to dim as he got out into the clear spring air and faced the reality of the city with all its movement and noise and color. But there was no change at all.

HE STOPPED at a street corner, waiting for the green light. He drew himself up to full height and sniffed deeply of the air, which was only moderately loaded with carbon monoxide at this time of morning. Why had he let a thing like this shake him so? People had hunches all the time; it was quite an ordinary thing, after all, when you stopped to think about it. He had no reason to feel apologetic, because he'd finally had one for the first time in his life.

But it wasn't any good. He knew he'd have lived out his full fourscore and ten without ever experiencing a genuine hunch, if it hadn't been for Magruder. All his life he'd laughed at hunches, and at the people who depended upon them for important decisions in their lives. Now, with one of his own, he felt like an unlucky prospector who'd sour-graped himself into believing there was no ore—only to come upon the biggest strike of all.

He stopped again in the middle of the block, and stepped back against the storefronts, a sudden new burden upon him. His face paled.

It was his habit to watch the crowds on the streets. Sometimes he counted a hundred of those going past in the opposite direction and estimated with a shallow regret that twenty-five of them would feel the death-grip of cancer. As many more would give way to failing hearts. There would be diabetes, infections, and accidents in decreasing proportions.

This always made him a little sad. Now, for the first time, he recognized how much he'd exulted in this private knowledge, and how superior he'd regarded himself because of it. It had been a power over his fellows—as if he, personally, were responsible for their fate.

With horror, he recognized something new. The passers-by were no longer an amorphous, faceless stream; they had become a procession of *individuals*.

THAT WOMAN in the red coat standing by the baby carriage—

As if in a nightmare, he found himself moving across the sidewalk toward her. "That tumor—" he said in a mild, hesitant voice; "it's so small now, it could probably be removed before metastasis—"

She stared at him in a moment of fright, then reassured herself by a glance at the passers-by. "I don't know you," she said with cold contempt, not at all alarmed.

Bascomb realized in dim horror what he had done. He touched his hat brim and glanced nervously about. "I beg your pardon," he said, backing away. "You *will* see your doctor, though, won't you—?"

His withdrawal gave her added courage. "I oughta call a cop! In broad daylight, too. And a woman with a six months old baby—can ya beat that?"

His heart was pounding heavily as Bascomb turned in full retreat. He rounded the corner and stopped in front of a cigar store window, watching the reflections in the glass to make sure he wasn't followed by an angry, insulting policeman.

WHEN HE was able to breathe easier, he faced the pedestrians again with the new awareness he possessed of his fellow men. Intuitively, he could correct the crude, statistical knowledge he'd been content with up to now. How ridiculous it was to be content merely with *how many* when it was possible to know *which ones.*

He glanced up sharply to the man standing next to him. The stranger was looking absently at a box of high-priced cigars, but his face was drawn into a warp of indecision.

"It won't work," Bascomb said quietly. It was almost impossible for him to keep from speaking. "The deal is rigged," he said, "and they're waiting for you to walk into the trap."

The man's face paled and then grew scarlet with rage. "What do you know about it?" he demanded. "Who are you?" He advanced threateningly and Bascomb was sure he'd have laid hands on him if the sidewalk hadn't been crowded.

"I'm a friend," said Bascomb in haste, backing again from this new encounter. "Take my word for it and don't sign the contract."

Then he darted away with a speed that shocked his system. The stranger attempted a short pursuit, but gave it up as ridiculous in the heavy pedestrian traffic. His mind was made up, however; though he would not have admitted it, the fantastic warning had tipped the decision for him.

Bascomb slowed as he found the steps of the Public Library, but he went up, two steps at a time. In the reading room, he settled by the window, keeping an eye open for signs of pursuit.

He had done a foolish thing. He would not pull that kind of stunt again. At least he'd try not to—the sudden impact of this sure, certain *knowing* was difficult to resist.

CHAPTER SEVEN

FOR ALMOST two hours Charles Bascomb sat there, apparently just staring through the window. But his mind was burning with the fury of the effort to evaluate the change within himself. He saw all his past life as a dark, empty grayness—a feeble reliance on somebody else, who relied on somebody else— If a man was wrong in statistical Society he could always fall back on his group, his school, "that's what they taught me", his insurance company, "everybody knows that", his firm—the bigger the cushion, the better.

It seemed impossible that that life was only as far away as this very morning, when he'd left the house, and that vision had come within these few hours.

It wasn't that sudden, of course. Magruder's pills and exercises had been working on him for days, now. Perhaps it took something like the encounter with Sprock to jar his intuitive faculty into action. At any rate, he would never be the same again. His life could never be the same.

The most immediate thing he had to take care of was calling off Hap Johnson's newspaper campaign against the Professor. After that, there would be time enough to determine what his relationship with Magruder would be.

But he already had an inkling of what would be necessary.

HE FOUND Hap in the *Courier* office looking unchanged from the time of his last visit. The reporter looked up, pleased as he saw Bascomb's face. "Pretty good story to start off with, don't you think?" he said. "The switchboard has taken seventy or eighty calls on it already. Most of them giving us kudos.

"It was a good story," Bascomb said, taking a seat by the worn desk. "It will have to stop, however."

"What—?"

Bascomb nodded. "I have found out something I didn't know before. Magruder is no fake; his stuff works."

"You said that before. The idea was to keep it from working."

"On me, I mean. I've found out how to use it in a different way than Magruder intended; it can be used constructively, not the way Magruder is doing."

Hap frowned in suspicion and puzzlement. "I don't get this," he said. "You mean you want to have things all love and kisses between you and Magruder now, and promote his phony self-development course instead of fight it?"

Bascomb shook his head. "I haven't quite figured out what ought to be done about Magruder. He's a crackpot—there seems no getting around that fact. Probably a senile condition; he's retired from the university you know. I suspect the full story is something like this: He stumbled on some bio-chemical concoction that would enormously improve a man's mental abilities—actually induce a genuine intuitive ability. He probably tried to sell his associates and superiors on it and was laughed at for his trouble. That would naturally sour him on all efforts to promote it honestly and professionally, so he became embittered and turned to this self-development business to promote it under cover.

"But with a difference. Where his initial impulse was no doubt to use his discovery for the benefit of mankind, he's now determined to destroy everything he can as a revenge for the rebuff by his colleagues."

"Which is a good enough reason why we should continue to blast him," said Hap.

BASCOMB shook his head. "No; in doing that, we would be running the risk of destroying the discovery itself. We can't take the chance; it's too valuable. The first thing necessary is to preserve Magruder himself until we can obtain control of his discovery and make sure it will be used properly. Then we can take steps to see that Magruder is prevented from taking out his bitterness against society; it's absolutely necessary to withdraw our attack on Magruder now."

Hap's look of suspicion deepened. "I don't see it. You are only theorizing about Magruder's background; and all I can see is that his system has been pretty effective—in taking you over onto his side! What makes you think that this intuitive thing is all to the good if it's used right—and that you can handle it better than Magruder?"

Bascomb told him about the morning's incidents with Sprock and the strangers on the street. He tried to describe his new outlook on the world.

"O.K. Tell me something about me," said Hap in quick challenge.

"Why, yes—" Bascomb said hesitantly. "You—"

He stopped.

"Go on," said Hap. "Should I take a bus or a taxi home tonight? Will it be safe enough to come to work tomorrow?"

Bascomb tried to speak. Nothing came. "There's nothing I can tell you," he said at last. "I haven't got it fully, and in a way I can control all the time. It's just at certain times, and certain circumstances; you've got to understand that, Hap."

"All I can see is that Magruder's got you over on his side. For my book, he's a dangerous charlatan who needs to be stamped out; and that goes double in view of what he's done to you. I don't know how he engineered such a switch, but you aren't the same man I knew a few days ago."

Bascomb tried again, from the beginning. But there was nothing he could say to convince Hap Johnson of his changed point of view—or rather, of the harmlessness of it.

The reporter stood up as Bascomb approached the door to leave. "I'm going to fight Magruder, because I think he's a menace to decent, ordinary-thinking people," he said. "And if you go over to his side, Charley, I'm going to fight you. too."

There was no hint of friendship in his eyes.

"I see," said Bascomb slowly. "Well, thanks, anyway, Hap; maybe we'll get together on this thing before it's over."

HE TRIED to assess Hap Johnson's intense hostility as he went out to the street again. The more he thought about it, the more incredible it seemed. Hap hadn't even been *that* hostile toward Magruder originally; he'd more or less gone along routinely, seeing Magruder as a crank to be suppressed. Now Bascomb felt that the reporter had become his own personal enemy because of the attempt to call off the campaign. He shook his head and gave up the problem for the present.

His inability to put on a demonstration for Hap troubled him, but he felt his explanation had been right. He had something that was growing within him; it couldn't be forced or pushed. It had to come at its own rate, and he was willing to give it time. But he couldn't afford to be backed into a corner like that again until it was fully matured.

Finally, he wanted desperately to talk to somebody who could understand him. He thought momentarily of Magruder himself, but that was out. He felt that he and the Professor were going to be very bitter enemies over exploitation of intuitive processes, and only one of them could survive that struggle.

There was no one—except Sarah.

HE GLANCED at the clock on the corner. She'd be startled to see him coming home in the middle of the day; and old Sprock would run a fever if he ever found out—perhaps even fire him. Somehow, that was becoming less and less important as the day went on.

Sarah greeted him with a smile, opening the door before he was halfway up the walk. "I thought you'd be on the earlier train," she said.

Bascomb stopped, then smiled back at her; he should have known.

They sat in the living room, and he told her about the events of the morning. He told of the interview with Sprock, and the sudden burst of intuitive knowledge that overwhelmed him. He told of the encounters with the strangers on the street, just as he'd told it to Hap Johnson. And he described the reaction of the reporter.

Sarah listened responsively, as if it were all something she'd heard before and had expected to hear again; but when he was through Bascomb realized that he hadn't come home merely for the purpose of telling her these things. He arose and stood by their modern picture window overlooking the landscaped back yard. There was still a great deal to say and he wasn't quite sure how to go about it.

"It must be that a statistician is essentially a coward," he said finally. "I've spent my life running—fleeing as hard as I could from contact with individual factors. I don't know why; maybe it was because I felt helpless in the presence of an individual—whether it was a figure or a human being.

"But in dealing with groups, and predicting their behavior—there was power in that!" He turned to Sarah, facing her motionless figure across the room. "Can you understand that, darling? Can you understand what it meant to be able to comprehend a mass of individuals when I was completely frightened by the randomness of a single one?"

"Yes—I can understand it," Sarah said softly.

"NOW, IT'S gone," Bascomb went on in a low voice. "The terror of an individual is gone—and so is the sense of power over any group whose action I can predict. It's more than my professional career that's involved; it's the basic postulates of my whole life. I can quit hiding behind my ridiculous little rows of black figures, my summations, my media, my extremes. I can quit being the absurd fool I have been all my life!"

Sarah shook her head. "If you had been a fool, you would never have been able to see what you have been doing. You have merely gained sight which you never had before—and you mustn't forget that you still live in a world of the blind."

"How close am I?" Bascomb said. "You're so far ahead of me—can you tell me how close I am to getting full use of my intuitive capacity so that I can depend on it?"

Sarah shook her head. "I can't even see the end of the road for myself; sometimes I think there may not be any. It may be like a skill that can grow and increase as long as you live. And I'm not so far ahead of you, either; not really. I never had very much; I was just willing to trust and use what I had. It works that way. The more you use it, the more reliable it becomes."

HE CROSSED the room and sat down beside her again. He told her his feeling about Magruder and his theoretical explanation for the Professor's behavior. "Magruder's found something with the potency of atomic energy—and he's using it to light a bonfire. It has to be taken out of his hands and put to proper use. That's my concern now—but I feel the need of more development for myself before trying to take it away from him."

"I think you're right in wanting to exploit his discovery, but I'm not sure Magruder's activities are entirely in error. After all, he brought it to your attention through these methods."

"Yes, but a direct approach would have been a whole lot more effective; and any good results are only incidental. His basic purpose is destructive. He told me so himself."

"What are you going to do?"

Bascomb shook his head. "I don't know. I thought maybe you could help me there. I try to think ahead on it, but I get nothing but fog and fuzz. I can't seem to grasp any plan of action for myself. I don't get that intuitive feel about anything except that I must protect Magruder from Hap Johnson right now, in order to save his discovery.

"Later, there can be lectures, courses, a school maybe—not the kind of thing Magruder has been doing, but a straightforward presentation showing what his actual discovery is and what it can do. That's the approach we'll make, I think."

"But there'll be effects that will certainly startle and shock people—"

"We'll prepare them; we'll lay it on the line and let them know exactly what to expect—not sneak up on them without any warning the way Magruder is doing."

"What about such things as your insurance business? It will be bankrupt in time."

"That's the obvious conclusion, but I don't think it's necessarily the right one—for the simple reason that insurance company people can also have the same advantage."

"IT WOULD be a stalemate then," said Sarah. "People would apply for policies only when they needed them, and the insurance companies would turn them down on the basis of knowing claims would soon be made."

"It would turn into a kind of savings and loan institution," Bascomb answered. "People could plan far enough ahead for coming emergencies. Insurance companies could cover them by accepting savings, and making loans for amounts beyond them—such loans being repayable in some manner. It's the only way it would ever work."

"But so many other things, too. There'll be the public schools, the courts and juries." She gave a small gasp. "There's Zad Clementi, Charles—"

Bascomb's mind shifted to thoughts of the alleged kidnap-murderer, whose trial had been headline news in their town for weeks. "Clementi—?" he said. Then the sad, sure intuitive awareness made itself felt in his mind. "Yeah," he said. "There's Clementi; he didn't do it, but they'll take a vote on it and decide to hang him for it. Twelve good men and true—in the statistical world you can multiply ignorance by a constant and get truth."

Sarah had straightened, her eyes staring through the window to the garden beyond. "We could help," she said in a whisper, "if we knew the right answer—"

Bascomb shook his head. "I can't get it; there's only the fog and fuzz. Have you got it?"

Sarah shook her head bitterly. "No—I don't know how to reach it yet. I wonder if it will be like this always—so many things you know exist, just beyond your fingertips?"

CHAPTER EIGHT

IN A KIND of fierce desperation, they returned to Magruder's manuals during the following evenings. They swallowed the green and orange and yellow and brown pills with conscious intensity, as if this would increase the potency of the chemicals.

They attended Magruder's lectures and drank up every precious word he spoke. Bascomb tried to shear through the overburden of wordage and digest the meat; Sarah refused to worry about this, taking it all at face value.

The children had been aware of some kind of strange, extracurricular activity on the part of their parents for some time. Now the sense of intensity grew somewhat frightening to them; but Charles Bascomb was not ready to admit them to an understanding of what was being attempted. He didn't know how he could make them understand fully enough to keep from resenting it. And then at other times, he wondered if they might already understand too well.

His own development progressed at a rate that was pleasing to Bascomb in spite of his impatience. After the first violent shock of becoming aware of intuitive powers, he restrained himself on the streets and on the train and wherever he had casual meeting with hordes of his fellow men. He steeled himself to walk by men who were dying and to sit near those who were headed for inevitable disaster—disaster and death that might be turned aside by even a small degree of insight.

The revolution in his own life he began to see in appalling proportions. He'd known that changes would be necessary; but the early estimates were revised upward in a continually widening spiral. He began to know periods of genuine fear as he saw the gap widening between the future and the past—but he would not have turned back, even if it were possible.

He had not changed his initial estimate of Magruder's person and methods, or the necessity of restricting his activities, but preservation of the discovery was the all-important concern right now; and anything that would lead to this end was fair enough.

HE CALLED at Magruder's hotel two weeks after the discovery of his own rising intuitive powers. Magruder, by that time, had been brought under indictment for practicing medicine without license—as a result of Hap Johnson's articles and a complaint based on Joe Archer's analysis of the colored pills. Skillfully, Hap had built up a powerful attack against all quacks and charlatans in the health and mental development field; and without leaving his paper open in any way for libel, he had directed public attention and sentiment towards Magruder and his course of lectures.

The Professor opened the door after Bascomb's first knock. "I was waiting for you."

And suddenly the enormity of his incredible oversight hit Bascomb between the eyes. How could he combat or deceive in any way a man who had the intuitive ability that Magruder must have? It was an impossibility!

How could he have overlooked this simple fact? And yet he had overlooked it completely.

"Are you feeling ill?" Magruder asked solicitously. "Can I get you anything?"

Bascomb shook his head. "I'm all right; just need to sit down. Over here by the window will be all right."

Magruder nodded and escorted him to the chair, then took one for himself. "It's good to see you again. I've been aware of you at the lectures, but you always get away so quickly I don't have a chance to even say hello."

"I've been reading about your trouble," said Bascomb a little thickly.

"That! It's nothing; it occurs all the time. All I have to do is make a delaying action until I finish the lectures. Then I'll pay my fine and be on my way."

"Do you think you'll get by with a fine?"

MAGRUDER frowned, his wrinkled face contorting like an old apple. "These newspaper articles have a rather unusual skill, coupled with an extraordinary amount of venom. I confess they do worry me, somewhat; you didn't know what you were starting."

Bascomb remained quite still. *Was there anything Magruder didn't know?*

He had admitted worry over the outcome of the indictment, however—as if that were still hidden from him. Bascomb wondered how it could be, what limits there were to intuition, anyway.

Bascomb said carefully, "I've changed my mind since our last meeting."

"I know," Magruder answered almost impatiently.

Bascomb swallowed hard. The only possible direction was straight ahead, regardless of what Magruder "knew".

"Then you must also know that my own intuition has begun to function," he said. "I didn't understand what you were talking about before; now I do. I want to go along with you."

"I know that, too," Magruder repeated, nodding. "I'll be delighted to have you, of course. There is only one additional item we need mention: the price."

"You said nothing about price."

"When we talked before, you weren't interested enough to warrant my quoting it. But now you need to know that it's going to cost you everything that has value to you as a member of a statistical society. Your present job; your career as a statistician—"

"I expected that."

"Your name; your position in the community; your home—everything, in fact, except your family. You have good fortune, indeed, in your wife."

Bascomb paled. "I don't understand," he murmured.

"You can't; not now. Understanding will come later. The important thing is that you are ready to begin. You value sufficiently the power of intuition to be willing to pay the price of everything Statistical Society offers. There is no doubt about that, is there?"

Bascomb looked across at the enigmatic Professor in staring silence. Nothing in his whole life had prepared him for so fantastic a conversation as this one. What did Magruder mean? How much did he actually know? If he could be so positive about some things, and yet have doubt about others, it was obvious he did not have hundred percent intuition. And one of the things he seemed not to know was Bascomb's own private intentions in this matter. If that were true—and Bascomb felt almost certain of it—then this talk of a fantastic "price" was just that—fantastic.

He had to gamble on it. He nodded his head slowly and said, "There is no doubt about it. I am ready to begin."

"Excellent!" exclaimed Magruder. He got to his feet energetically. "There are a good many things I have to show you. This indictment business is going to interfere considerably, and you can be a great help to me within a short time—"

HOURS LATER, Bascomb had a substantial lead in the direction he wanted to go. Magruder gave no sign of doubting Bascomb's good faith, or sensing his real purpose.

He explained the source of his medication—a small private capsule company—and gave Bascomb authority to place orders with a letter of introduction that would validate those orders. He admitted the false front of gobbledygook pseudo-scientific terms in his lectures.

"That's the way it has to be done," he said confidentially. "The public would never swallow the actual facts. They'd rather have corporeal vibrations and ethereal streams, than try to understand that men made a mistake in the dawn of history which we now have to correct."

"But what kind of teaching is that?" Bascomb demanded in spite of himself. "How can they ever learn what intuition really is by such methods?"

Magruder glanced sidewise at him. "How does a baby learn to see, or to smell, or to feel? Intuition's like that. First order functions can't be *taught*. They are blueprinted in the germ plasm from ages past, and the psyche reads the plans in the dark schoolroom of the womb. There, it learns how to make its own heart beat, and when it comes into the world, how its eyes are to function—and its lungs, stomach, and intuition. No—you don't teach those things."

"But what do you do, then? Something happens—something happened to teach me how to use intuition."

"DID IT? I think not. You learned how yourself after I assisted in removing some of the obstacles imposed by a Statistical Society. The exercises free the imagery mechanisms of your mind, teach your body that it need not abhor certain inherent functions. The pills react biochemically to inhibit the fear component attached to these functions. A wholly artificial fear, you understand, which has been laboriously attached by Society.

"That is all that is possible to do. Teaching is a greatly over-rated activity. It is obviously nothing more than extracting an agreement—sometimes to good ends, sometimes to bad. But it's always applied to second order effects, the use of a function—not the function itself.

"Self-learned items such as breathing, heart circulation, intuition, artistic creation, and ten thousand others can be suppressed by forces which may be stronger than the urge to live and grow. If the suppression has not already caused the death of the body—or the soul—it may be possible to remove the suppression, but still the organism must do its own learning in the first order field of living, growing, creating.

"In our activity we do nothing but remove the suppressors."

Bascomb made no comment. He cringed slightly before the Professor's reflection on the many years spent in achieving his place as a scholarly statistician; but it was heavy going following the physiological and psychological theories into which Magruder now plunged. Bascomb tried to stay with it, taking copious notes to refresh his memory and to check against standard texts later.

WHEN THE interview was finally over, Bascomb felt he was well on his way. Reaching the street after leaving Magruder's suite, only one puzzle remained to plague his mind insistently.

The price.

Magruder saw disaster ahead for him; but nothing could be clearer than Bascomb's own intuitive knowledge that he was on the right track—and Sarah verified it wholeheartedly.

Could two people, with functioning intuitive powers, get opposing answers to the same problem?

The answer was obviously no—provided there was any validity to intuitive knowledge at all. That left two possibilities: Magruder's intuitive power was less than Bascomb's own; or Magruder had no knowledge whatever of Bascomb's real intentions and this made the difference in their view of the future.

Bascomb contented himself with this latter answer; he wasn't entirely satisfied with it, but there was no other in sight. And he knew he was right in what he was doing. There was no question of it, no sliver of doubt.

HE HAD decided that Hap Johnson's articles could be useful, after all, in keeping Magruder too occupied to pay too close attention to Bascomb's failure to follow instructions—if only it didn't turn heavily against the discovery itself.

Bascomb was thinking this the next morning when he opened the paper and Magruder's picture slapped him in the eye. The Professor had been arrested during the previous afternoon. He had not put up bail—which was set at an unreasonably high fifteen thousand dollars. He was securely in jail.

The news was disconcerting. Bascomb hadn't wanted anything like this to befall the Professor; yet it put him safely out of the way, and left a free hand to inaugurate a sane program. It would be all to the good as long as it restrained the professor's destructive activities—without destroying his discovery. It seemed to Bascomb a good indicator that he, not the Professor, was right. He had an intuitive feeling that this was so; it meant he had to get started—and quickly.

There was the question of Bascomb's job with New England. At first, he had considered leaving it forthwith—but that was mere crude logic that led to such a conclusion. Intuitively, now, he recognized the necessity of remaining.

First of all, he needed the money it provided. But in addition, the company represented an institution he had come to love; he didn't intend to see it scuttled. The obvious course was to take a hand in the inevitable transition. Men like Sprock would need a great deal of help during that difficult time.

As SOON as he reached the office that morning, Bascomb requested Hadley to make a check on the batch of policies he'd warned Tremayne and Sprock about. There was no waiting; Hadley had the information already at hand, having started a one-man project to discover anomalies.

"Five of those you mentioned have made claims," he said, and was pleased at Bascomb's resulting smile. But on second thought his pleasure turned to wonder. How could Bascomb have known what ones to ask for?

"Get me the papers," said Bascomb; "I want to add them to my study."

He checked them over. It would have been nice if the remaining one had come in, but this was good enough. One death claim; two accidents, and two liabilities. He took the sheaf of papers and walked down the hall to Sprock's office.

The vice-president glanced up belligerently as the secretary ushered Bascomb in. "I was about to call you," he said. He ruffled a handful of papers in front of him and lowered bushy eyebrows. "It's time we did some more talking."

Bascomb's heartbeat quickened a trifle, and then he knew that Sprock already had a report on the claims. He hadn't ignored the prediction, after all!

Smiling, Bascomb took the offered chair. "I think we both have the same thing in mind," he said.

"All right, talk!" The vice-president commanded.

"I wasn't honest with you when I was here the other day," said Bascomb with deliberation. "I told you I had predicted these claims on the basis of a new mathematical formula I had developed. That wasn't true."

"Then why did you tell me such a cock and bull story!" Sprock roared.

"Because I felt you wouldn't be likely to believe the genuine truth. Now that I have the proof I can tell you. I predicted those claims simply because of the ability—in and of myself, without the help of any formula of any kind—to do so. Such an ability is sometimes called intuition."

"Bascomb, I warned you the last time you were in here—"

"These policyholders have the same kind of ability: that's why they were able to predict their own immediate need of insurance."

SPROCK'S face clouded even further; his fist clenched the papers to a wad. "You can't possibly believe I'm going to accept a fool story like that!"

Bascomb waited. He held out the claim papers. "These must be explained," he said.

Sprock's silence seemed interminable; he was so immobile he seemed scarcely alive. Only the faint movement of his thin chest and the rapid shifting of his cold blue eyes to Bascomb's face and back to the papers betrayed animation.

Finally, he spoke again. "Go on," he said. "I believe you; I have to believe you."

"There'll be thousands of these," said Bascomb. "You are thinking it means the end, if enough people find themselves able to do what these few have done. That's not necessarily true. I—and others like me—can work from this end, detecting such applications.

"But it means that we must have a new policy; this is what I came to see you about. We'll have to issue a policy whose benefits are based on the term, which it has run. We'll issue them only to people like these." He patted the pile of claims. "That will show them the system works both ways and will discourage their attempts to bring a run on us; after that, we'll need a new kind of program." In detail, he explained his proposal for a savings and loan system, which would serve the needs of intuitionists and keep the company solvent.

When he was through, Sprock's expression remained unchanged. "I will take your recommendations under advisement," he said. "I'll have to discuss these short claims with our Board. But later, you and I will have much more talking to do about this newfound ability. I think there needs to be considerable explanation about its sudden appearance in epidemic form!"

"Any time that is convenient, sir," said Bascomb, rising. "I can tell you whatever you wish to know about it."

HE WAS a trifle disappointed that Sprock did not demand further explanation at the moment but this was overshadowed by his elation at Sprock's unwilling, yet definite acceptance of the reality of intuition. The first great step had been taken.

Later in the day he took a second, smaller step. He called Hadley in and with a confidential air that thrilled the junior statistician he explained about intuition. Hadley took it with difficulty; he was well on the way to solidification in his statistical mold. But when Bascomb offered personally to teach him the methods of intuition he expressed effusive thanks.

These were beginnings; but a bold program of expansion was necessary now to take advantage of Magruder's difficulty, and his own possession of the basic data on intuition.

From Magruder's secretary—who was now out of a job and didn't care much about the Professor's affairs in the first place—he obtained a list of those registered for the course of lectures. He prepared a letter explaining that he was in a position to explain Magruder's difficulty with the law and replace the hocus-pocus of his lectures with an honest exposition of the principles of man's intuitional powers and how to attain them.

He prepared a second letter, which went to a large, select group of personal friends, business associates, and clients of New England. In this he outlined the occurrence of anomalies in human wisdom and insight and explained briefly the role of intuition in men's affairs. He invited them to attend a series of discourses and instruction on how to improve their personal intuitive abilities.

HE CHANGED the location from Magruder's meeting place in order to eliminate as much as possible all association with the Professor's quackery and nonsense. He was going to give out the data in a strictly scientific, straight-from-the-shoulder manner that would be bound to appeal to people of intellect and logical thinking. People who could understand the tremendous responsibility toward society, which was involved in obtaining use of the intuitive faculties of the mind. With such a class of people initially in possession of full intuition there would be no risk of the panic and ruin that Magruder's program was deliberately designed to induce.

He felt good about the whole thing; it was intuitively correct. Sarah agreed that it was. Her only worry was in regard to Magruder. "We ought to do something to help," she said. "After all, he's the one responsible for bringing these principles to light. We owe him for that. And those newspaper articles are getting people so inflamed against him that he's liable to get a sentence of twenty years in jail, for things he didn't have the remotest chance of doing."

Bascomb himself was still uncertain about the position of Magruder. It worried him, too; particularly since there was no intuitive insight either of them could get regarding him.

"After this thing gets rolling," he promised. "I'll have a talk with him and see if something can't be done. I'll see Cummings the D. A., too. I used to sit next to him at Club."

Bascomb was quite aware that he was going to distribute pills just as Magruder had done, which was the immediate cause of Magruder's arrest; but he knew there was no risk to himself in this. In the Professor's case it had been just an excuse to lay hands on him: with a straightforward approach there would be no such complication.

CHAPTER NINE

CHARLES and Sarah Bascomb were elated by the sight of the first night crowd filling up the hall. Logic had told them they were getting a place much too big. But it was just right.

The crowd was divided about equally between Bascomb's friends and business people, and the group from Magruder's course. Bascomb was continually surprised by his own lack of apprehension concerning the reactions of both groups. It would be difficult to wean Magruder's people away from corporeal vibrations; and he knew the business people would not take kindly to the idea that statistics was a feeble tool to be used only in the absence of a more profound and positive intuition. Yet he felt completely secure in what he was about to do.

The feeling persisted, even when Hap Johnson walked in and took a seat at the rear of the hall. Bascomb admitted to himself he was shaken when he looked out and saw the reporter's entrance. He hadn't invited, Hap, and had no idea how he had got wind of the meeting. But it didn't matter, he thought; nothing that the *Courier* might print could possibly alter the intuitive assurance he felt.

He stepped out between the curtains on the platform. He was aware of the stares of surprise, curiosity, challenge, and occasional contempt. He smiled confidently and held up a hand to quiet the perfunctory applause.

"It was probably no small surprise to those of you who know me," he said, "to read my invitation to this gathering. I am gratified that so many of you took the trouble to accept and be here tonight.

"What I have to say will sound strange to all of you. Some of you will be thoroughly outraged—even as I was when I first encountered this information. I hope no one will be so outraged or disbelieving that he will consider it beneath his dignity to test the validity of these facts for himself—also as I have done."

GINGERLY, then, as if edging carefully into cold, deep water, Bascomb spoke of the historical evidence for the existence of intuition as it might be familiar to his audience. He modified Magruder's exposition considerably, omitting the Professor's far-fetched theories that went back to the dawn of civilization. He reminded his listeners of instances, which they could believe, in which intuition had proven superior to all other forms of knowledge as a basis for action.

They listened, but he could see they weren't liking it. Magruder's group was obviously contemptuous of so prosaic a term as intuition; they wanted strong meat—corporeal vibrations. The businesspeople were disgusted; Bascomb could read in their faces the thoughts he himself had had, not so long ago.

Somehow he wasn't getting it over; he was trying to be reasonable and scientific, but his listeners were cold to his exposition.

"How much would it be worth to know," he said, "which one out of many possible lines of action was most likely to succeed? How much would it be worth to know which man out of a group could best do a job—or which product out of many thousands was not up to specified quality? You who are executives, personnel managers, quality control experts— what would it be worth to you to have infallible insight in your profession instead of mere assurance that your error will not be greater than a stated amount?

"Statistics can never give you anything more than this assurance. Intuition, properly applied, can give you positive knowledge."

IN HIS backward-looking moments he never quite understood why he dared the argument he brought up next. Certainly, his planned discourse didn't call for it; but the apathy of the group made him a little desperate, he thought afterward.

"Think of the significance in our judicial processes," he said. "We never *know* in many instances whether a man is actually guilty of a crime or not. We take a ballot and *vote* him guilty or innocent, and our concept of justice and our lust for vengeance are satisfied.

"We have seen in recent days how this functions in our own city. We have voted a man guilty of the worst possible crime. There were good, sound, logical reasons for such a vote. He was a poor, unlettered devil who aroused no one's sympathy, so who could regret if an error were made? Besides, he was the janitor in the apartment house where the victim lived, and she was found stuffed in the furnace to which only he was supposed to have access.

"But I know that Zad Clementi is innocent of this crime!"

FOR SHEER emotional reaction, he might as well have set off a charge of dynamite in their midst. There was no physical response, but he felt the hostile flare in their minds like a bright, silent flame.

There was not a man or woman in the audience who didn't believe Zad Clementi was a justly condemned murderer.

Bascomb recognized his error the moment he closed his mouth, and he was appalled. Whatever had caused him to bring up such an argument? He was acting like a fool, letting their apathy rattle him; where was his intuitive assurance regarding his course of action?

It was there, silent, reassuring, commending him for having done well.

And for the first time since it came, he began to doubt.

He was *not* doing well; he had made a blunder that had alienated his listeners beyond all repair.

But he tried to make repairs. For another full hour he tried valiantly to convey something of his own sense of faith in the intuitive powers of Man. With that faith so severely shaken, however, he had no ability to persuade others.

When some of those in the back rows began getting up to leave, he knew his chance was gone.

Not all of them were ready to walk out on him, however. Some wanted to talk it over, and insisted on the scheduled question and answer period. They didn't want to know about the methods of gaining intuitive understanding; they wanted to tell him what they thought about the things he'd already said.

It grew boisterous and vicious; he left the platform in defeat.

AS IF HE had forgotten where he lived, or didn't want to go there, he drove through town and along its outskirts and suburbs in a mazelike pattern. Beside him, Sarah remained silent, waiting for him to be the first to speak.

He did, finally. He said bitterly, "How do you suppose I ever got suckered into a thing like that? I must have been crazy the past few weeks—completely off my nut! Intuition—!"

"You don't believe it's real any more?" asked Sarah quietly.

"As real as it's always been—a chance hunch now and then. With just as much chance of being wrong as right!"

"What about the policies?"

"What about them? I'll find that statistical formula I bragged about to Sprock and explain them! The ones that won't fit—well, the old idea of a hunch is as good as any explanation. I'll buy it. But what a fool Magruder made out of me, with his Yogi tricks and slick performance! I'll bet he isn't even Magruder—"

"What about Myersville?"

"Who knows—it has nothing to do with this."

"And Sloane and his soap failure?"

"He's probably got his trouble ironed out by now."

"And you felt it so strongly yourself—that is was real and this was the way to go."

Bascomb's lips compressed tightly before he answered. "I've seen the same thing in backwoods religious meetings, too."

"I still feel somehow that tonight was not a loss," said Sarah.

"It wasn't," Bascomb answered grimly. "It put me back on the track. What if I'd quit New England first? But there's still Sprock." He grimaced painfully. "Tomorrow I have to see Sprock and do the Most Humble Grand Salaam."

HE NEVER got the chance; he suspected he wouldn't when he saw the paper before breakfast the following morning. The international news was light, and his own picture was on the front page, neatly framed by Magruder's on one side and Zad Clementi's on the other.

The caption declared: *"Mathematician Computes Clementi Innocence."*

The story described him as a disciple of Magruder, taking over the Professor's work while the latter languished in jail, unable to provide bail on charges of medical practice without license. It told in great detail and with considerable accuracy the things Bascomb had said about intuition and the possibility of gaining skill in its use.

The story was written by Hap Johnson.

Near the end, Hap said; *"All this reminds your reporter about the old story of the tired bailiff who was asked to go out for about the nine hundredth time to get the belaboring jurors something to eat. He's the one, you remember, who came back with eleven meals and a bale of hay.*

"Well, we can all be thankful that a certain insurance statistician wasn't on the Clementi jury. We've had clean-cut justice done on this case, a thing our courts and the citizens of Landbridge can be proud of. But we'll tell you: if anyone still cares to make a gift of a bale of hay at this particular date, your reporter will see that it's properly delivered."

It sent a stunning wave of hurt through Bascomb as he read it. Hap Johnson had been his friend. This bitterness was something he did not understand; he gave up trying.

On his desk, when he reached the office, there was a note for him to appear in the office of vice-president Sprock. Bascomb caught furtive glances of those beyond the glass walls of his office as he read it. Obviously they'd seen the morning papers.

Hadley hadn't, apparently, for he came in brightly, almost on Bascomb's heels. "Here's the last of the policies you asked about, Mr. Bascomb," he said. "Bheuner's Hardware Store. It burned to the ground last night."

That must have been in the second section, which Bascomb hadn't read. He stood staring, long after Hadley had left, at the two papers on his desk: the order from Sprock, and the claim from Bheuner. The hardware man hadn't lost any time, he thought.

But it would do no good to call it to Sprock's attention now; his case was lost, as far as New England was concerned. He left the claim paper on his desk and walked slowly down the hall.

THE VICE-PRESIDENT was surprisingly direct and to the point. He outlined briefly the history of the insurance business, particularly that of New England. He dwelt at moderate length on the sacredness of the obligations incurred by the Company in behalf of the Policyholders. He went most heavily into the personal qualifications required of the ones chosen to stand vigil over that enduring trust.

But the thing of greatest significance was his parting shot: "I shall see to it personally, Bascomb, that no firm in this field ever considers your name on its roster without knowing the true facts of your fantastic attempt to besmirch the entire insurance institution in America! Intuition! Good day, Mr. Bascomb."

He returned along the hall to his own office. Blackballed—he had no doubts that Sprock would and could do it.

He had thirty days coming if he wanted it, but he declined. He told Sprock he'd finish up at once, if that was all right; it was. He turned over his current studies to Wardlaw, Assistant Statistician. He cleaned out his desk and said a stiff goodbye to the office associates who didn't suddenly have to go down the hall for a break as they saw he was about ready.

That was it. He and New England were through. As he turned his back on the building, he was aware that this fact had not sunk thoroughly into all his cells. A certain part of him had no doubt that he would be coming this way again in the morning. It would be a bitter struggle when that certain part attained full awareness.

SARAH WAS not surprised. They had discussed it at breakfast, and she had told him it was going to happen. He had believed her, but hoped for some miracle to prove her wrong—to prove all her intuitive hunches wrong for the rest of their lives.

It wouldn't be bad, however, he told her; he'd start looking in the morning. He might have to go farther away, but there wouldn't be much trouble for a man of his experience. He didn't tell her of Sprock's threat.

He did little the next day except write some letters asking for interviews. He went to a public stenographer in town to do this, and came home early—and the height of thirteen-year-old Mark's wails of rage and discomfort.

These were coming from the direction of the bathroom, where Bascomb found Sarah busy with soap and water and bandages. His oldest boy's eye was tightly closed. Cuts and bruises decorated the rest of his face and his upper torso.

Bascomb wanted to make it light, but he saw Sarah's face and changed his intended tone. "What was it all about?" he asked evenly.

MARK GLANCED up, hesitant; he turned to his mother. "It's all right," she said grimly.

"Down at school—" said Mark. "All the kids—I told them they couldn't say things like that and tried to make 'em shut up. But I couldn't lick the whole school."

"What were they saying?" Bascomb asked.

"That you are a Communist. They went around singing it kind of: Bascomb's dad's a Red man; that sort of thing. Then Art Slescher wrote on the boards in all the classes before I got there: *Name a dirty Commie*. I got him after school."

Bascomb looked at Sarah, his face blanched. They didn't speak.

Later, when the children were in bed, they tried to talk about it. "We can't go on bucking something like that forever," Sarah said.

"It won't be forever," Bascomb snapped, more irritably than he intended; "I mean, it will die down after while. You know how these newspaper stories go. They pin a guy to the cross with scandal, and in a week even his next door neighbors have forgotten about it."

"Not this." Sarah shook her head. "It hasn't even got a good start, it's going to build bigger and bigger. Mark's experience isn't the only one."

"What else?"

"I overheard talk at the store while I was shopping today. Two women on the other side of grocery island. They thought I'd gone away. One mentioned your name. Said her daughter had a friend who'd heard you were caught molesting some high school girls one night—that it was no wonder you were defending a man like Clementi."

BASCOMB buried his face in his hands and groaned with helpless despair and rage. "Such a little thing to begin with— How in Heaven's name did it lead up to this? I hope they hang Magruder!" He looked up. "It's going to be hell to live with while it lasts, but time will make a difference."

"Not in this." Sarah shook her head again; "it will only grow worse."

"Then what are we to do! We've got our home here. It's our community as much as those gossiping old biddies'— those mentally twisted kids—"

"It's going to force us out, Charles; we can't live here any longer. The sooner we prepare to leave, the better we'll be. Put the house up for sale tomorrow."

Only then, for the first time in many days, did Bascomb remember Magruder's strange words, and it hit him like a blow in the stomach. *"It's going to cost you everything—your present job, your whole career—your good name—your position in the community; your home—"*

Magruder had said that; and every word of it was coming true.

But there was time and a way to save things yet. "We're not moving out before a thing of that kind," he said; "there're ways of licking it."

"At the price of our own destruction!"

"It's always been expensive to fight against insane prejudice, but the world would be a hell of a place to live in if a few of us didn't try.

"Tell Mark to not get involved in any more fistfights; tell him that when the others accuse me of being a Communist, he's to agree. He's to tell them I've got a pipeline straight to Moscow. Kruschev himself appointed me, and I'm planning to wipe out the President and his Cabinet next month.

"Tell the neighborhood biddies the same thing. Walk up and ask their advice on what to do with a husband you catch every week or two with sixteen-year old girls right in your own house. That'll shut them up after a while.

"And then—we're staying; we're staying right here and we'll find out who did the murder Clementi is accused of. We'll ram it down their throats until it chokes every one of the lying, sadistic gossipers!"

"We have nothing but an intuitive sense about Clementi— and you've rejected that. So possibly the jury was right, after all."

BASCOMB remained staring straight ahead of him to the figured pattern on the opposite wall; it seemed as if he hadn't heard her. Then slowly his lips parted. "No," he said. "I've rejected everything Magruder induced me to believe about intuition, but Clementi's innocence doesn't depend on that. Our feelings about him were merely random chance, let us say, but logic convinces me we were right in that one thing. I've gone back and read the accounts of the trial. The evidence is ridiculous; they haven't given him a chance. And I think it's because there's someone who's being protected."

CHAPTER TEN

IT WAS A noble and virtuous gesture. Bascomb felt Sarah would commend him and agree to stick valiantly by him. Instead, she got up and paused in the center of the room. She gave him a single backward, almost-contemptuous look. "You are being an idiotic fool!" she said. "A pebble can't stop a fifty ton boulder rolling down a hill." She strode off in the direction of the bedroom.

A week later, Charles Bascomb was convinced she was right. Mark was in the hospital to get an arm set after it had been broken when the mob piled on him at school. Sarah had been read out of the two ladies clubs she belonged to; and the minister of their Church had informed her he had made different arrangements in the baby-sitting round robin, which had been worked out during services. Sarah wouldn't need to bother with it any more.

Bascomb had found his car painted a screaming red—including all the glass—when he got off the train at the end of the week to drive home. The same night their front windows were broken with slingshots; and when they got up, they found a crude hammer and sickle painted on the front door.

In the city he'd not been able to get a single job interview during the entire time.

Bascomb visited the local suburban real estate office in the early morning. By afternoon he had a sale—at a four thousand-dollar loss, which the agent assured him was the best he could do in the light of the jinxed condition of the property.

Once agreeing to defeat, it was impossible for Bascomb to get out too soon. He didn't know where they were going, but as soon as all arrangements for storage and forwarding of their personal goods had been made he turned the car west.

Slivers of red paint still showed next to the rubber gasket of the windshield; but the new paint job on the car symbolized the only thing he was taking with them, hope.

He didn't know where they were going. He was still stunned by the events of past days. The uncontrolled viciousness and brutality of the attacks against his family were unexplainable. Even the police had expressed apathy toward his complaints. A city had turned against him.

And for what? he asked himself continually, over and over again. There was no rational explanation. His single statement of defense for Clementi had set if off. But that must be only the trigger. Where was the main explosive force of the catastrophe! He didn't know. All he was sure of was that his townsmen seemed to have suddenly gone insane.

THEY CROSSED New York in easy stages, and stopped late that night at a Pennsylvania tourist lodge. Mark's arm was giving him pain. Neither Chuck, nor Darcie, the youngest, lying across his lap asleep, was enjoying the ride. They were running from a terror that wouldn't show its proper face.

It was there that they heard the newscast as they turned on the small radio in the lodge.

Police are looking for a once-respected insurance executive now fleeing with his family from the consequences of an incredible wave of criminal attacks. Charles Bascomb—dark green Buick—six girls all under age—license number—"

"Come on," said Bascomb. "It must have been on earlier; I noticed the clerk watching closely while I wrote down our license number—"

They turned out of the drive, even as the clerk came out of the office to witness their unexplained departure. Sarah saw him turn and run inside. "He's phoning the police," she said.

There was no hysteria, or even despair, Bascomb recalled later as he turned the car onto the highway and kept it moving. A kind of calm seemed to have settled over them all. The children were quiet, and Sarah sat as if she had confidence that Bascomb knew exactly what he was doing.

As if he actually did, he slowed at a dark intersection and turned off on a secondary highway. "We'll have to keep off the main roads," he said. "This one ought to take us where we're going."

No one asked where that was; at the moment Bascomb didn't think to inquire in his own mind just what he meant by his words. He just kept driving. About midnight he pulled up at a small country crossroads community. A single lighted sign: *Hotel* shown in the whole village.

"We'll be all right here," Bascomb said with assurance; "we'll try to get some rest and get out early in the morning."

THEY WENT south and west, avoiding the main highways rounding the Michigan shoreline. No one viewed them with any more suspicion than any ordinary family of tourists; no siren-screaming cars rocketed along side them. Just once did they catch a repeat of the news broadcast mentioning the police pursuit.

When Bascomb abruptly turned the car to a northerly course, he had a momentary impulse to stop and check the road map and ask himself why the devil he was heading this way. But he didn't stop; he merely slowed for an instant— then stepped on the gas and settled a little more comfortably behind the wheel. He'd known it all along, of course.

Where else would they be going but to Myersville—the town that burned television sets in the square?

THEY ARRIVED very late. The headlights of the car showed a neat village of white; green-trimmed houses. There appeared to be only a single hotel, and they drew up before it, after driving the length of the town and returning. As they walked into the small lobby a man got to his feet from a nearby leather chair and advanced with outstretched hand. He was smiling broadly.

"I've been waiting all evening for you," Professor Magruder said.

Sarah Bascomb walked toward him with an answering smile and accepted his hand. But Charles stopped short and stared at the little wizened man who was at the root of all his troubles.

He'd felt there was safety in their flight west. When Bascomb turned north, he knew he'd been subconsciously aware from the beginning that they'd end up in Myersville.

But by no twist of backward calculation could he admit that seeing Magruder was anything but an unexpected shock. Magruder was the last person in the world he wanted to meet.

"How did you get here?" he demanded.

"Flew," said Magruder easily. "The judge threw out the charges in the preliminary hearing, and let me go the day you left. I tried to get in touch with you, but you were a little too early for me. I knew I'd find you here."

"And just how did you know that?" Bascomb said belligerently.

Magruder smiled again. "How did you know Myersville was the place to come to?"

He refused to say another word about the subject of their past relationship. While he accompanied them to the dining room, and to a meal that seemed to have been waiting for them, he told about the town, its peacefulness and opportunity for full living, which he was sure they would enjoy. He spoke of other, incidental, things, but the word intuition was not mentioned that night.

He led them directly to their rooms afterward.

"We have to register," Bascomb explained.

"That has been taken care of," said Magruder. "After all, we run the place."

Bascomb knew by then it would be useless to ask the identity of "we".

THE CHILDREN had never seen the Professor, of course, and had heard his name only when it slipped in their presence. But they struck up an immediate friendship. At the breakfast table the following morning the Professor proved an unexpected adeptness with sleight-of-hand tricks, riddles, and stories that kept the children enthralled.

Bascomb, however, was more absorbed in an inspection of his fellow diners; he was used to seeing occasionally an individual lie mentally classified as a "character"—but never in such numbers as this. The hotel seemed to be full of them.

Magruder was watching him, he discovered after a time. The children and Sarah had turned to their meal, and the Professor said, "That's Shifty you're watching across the room. He's a great man in a poolroom. While pool isn't as popular as it once was, he handles dirty pictures, too. That gives him a good following in the high-school crowd, where he specializes in pushing our stuff. The kids think they've been on a genuine reefer jag when they get through."

"I'd like to know what the devil you're talking about," said Bascomb testily.

"Marty, over there, works the racing crowd. He gives them a system that really sends them flipping—but they pick the ponies right too. They wouldn't let go of Marty for all the uranium in Utah.

"Then the fellow next to him is Doc Simmons; he's a chiropractor. Has a nice little practice among neurotic females of the upper bracket in Chicago. Across the table is Doc Bywater—we have a lot of Docs here—who is behind the ads you see in the little magazine sometimes. You know: *cure piles in ten days or your money back.* Or: *prostrate sufferers, get relief overnight.* That sort of thing. He gives them a dilly of a routine, and, of course, it works one hundred percent of the time. He's got a warehouse full of testimonials."

"It makes absolutely no sense at all!" Bascomb exclaimed.

ALL RIGHT, then, I'll tell you." Magruder had been eating as he talked; now he arose, finished with breakfast while Bascomb hadn't touched a thing. Bascomb got up with him, however, and went out to the broad porch of the hotel and sat down facing the small unbusy main street of the town.

"Peaceful place, isn't it?" said Magruder. He pointed to a dark spot on the gravel of the town square a block away. "That's where they burned the television sets; it must have been quite a show.

"But you wanted to know what this was all about, didn't you? That shouldn't be very hard, actually, because you already know—"

"I don't know a thing," Bascomb cried. "Who are the 'we' you referred to last night? Who are the people you pointed out in the dining room—what's the meaning of their nonsensical activities?"

"The first thing you need to comprehend," said Magruder slowly and carefully now, "is that intuition does *not* provide you with a superman intellect in the logical, statistical world you have lived in all your life.

"Intuition is an entirely different breed of cat, a *non*-logical means of arriving at conclusions about the world. Remember that the world and its problems remain the same. Sometimes the answers are the same, too; most of them are considerably better. But the change of method sometimes tends to make the whole picture—the world of your reality, its problems, your personal inter-relations—all of these often look so different that you think you've suddenly dropped down on another world.

"Non-logical has come to be synonymous with irrational or crazy—a piece of sheer propaganda put out by a system struggling tooth and nail, so to speak, to prevent recognition of another and better system. When shifting from one to the other you may be inclined to discount some of the features of the new."

BASCOMB SNORTED in disgust. "If you're trying to tell me I had any sense of intuition at work you can save your breath. The one time I depended on it in full confidence, it nearly destroyed me. It wiped out everything I've built up so far—home, job, community relationship. I'm even wanted by the police, I hear. Heaven only knows how that will turn out!"

"No—I think Charles Bascomb knows that it will turn out all right. The hysteria will pass; the charges will be dropped and forgotten. There will be no continued pursuit and harassment from that quarter.

"I'm quite sure you know also that your intuition did not fail you. It was working accurately to bring you with optimum speed to the new circumstances which will give you maximum satisfaction in life."

"You're crazy! I took your pseudo-scientific nonsense, hook, line, and sinker, and determined I *would* base a new life on it. My wife agreed with me. Everything went wrong; you evidently know what happened."

"And you recall, also, that I predicted this would be the course of events? It had to be. You were following a strongly working intuitive faculty, and it was leading you along an optimum path.

"There's one trait of intuition that makes it a little hard for a statistically bred and educated man to stomach. Intuition is completely ruthless. If reaching a certain goal involves a pathway through bear-traps and hellfire, intuition makes no allowances for logical objections to these obstacles. It takes you through; that's what happened in your case."

"I hope you're not trying to tell me it was intuitionally desirable that I be run out of town with my reputation destroyed!"

MAGRUDER NODDED. "That's exactly the case," he said. "You had accepted your intuitive faculty as a prime motivator at the moment you recognized it actually existed. Not everyone does that, you understand, but you did—hook, line, and sinker, as you say.

"It was therefore very easy for it to assume a very high functioning level, and replace a considerable mass of logical reasoning. But even so, it was still comparatively embryonic in development—with the result that you were somewhat in the position of a man trying to ride two horses wanting to go in opposite directions.

"You permitted intuition to operate, but you tried to evaluate its results logically."

"An intuitionist has no desire for status in the community, I suppose! No need for a sound, stable reputation and solid family life!"

Magruder grimaced impatiently. "I suppose it's difficult to shuck off the lifelong habit of trying to generalize from a single specific incident. You'll learn, however—

"Your case has nothing to do with what intuitionists in general desire or do not desire. For you, your intuition determined an optimum course of action with the precision of Natural Law. For *you*, not for anybody else. For you."

"Is there any purpose in it that can be understood by my simple logical mind, then?" Bascomb asked bitterly.

"OF COURSE. It is simply that you had to be *driven* out of your niche in a statistical society, or you would not have gone. That represents an almost unbelievable reflex activity of the intuition, which *cannot* be understood in logical terms. It saw, so to speak, that you were desirous of utilizing intuition; but it also saw that you would never renounce sufficiently the statistical way of life you had built up so solidly. It saw, therefore the necessity of destroying the impediment in order to permit you to realize your basic intuitive choice of an intuitive life. So it set up the chain of circumstances—it led *you* to set them up—to destroy your position in statistical society, and thereby free you for the fuller life you had already chosen but could not otherwise obtain.

"You'll get used to that kind of operation after while; I'll admit it shakes you pretty hard the first few times it goes into operation!"

"It's absolutely—"

Bascomb didn't finish with the word "insane", which was on the tip of his tongue. He suddenly sat very still, staring across the quiet Main Street of Myersville. In the vault of his mind, a page seemed to have turned, and a previous opacity was flooded with a brilliance of light. He felt a trembling within the fibers of his being, that was at once both a joy and an apprehension.

Every word of Magruder's last statements was true!

HE SAW it now—and understood how he could not possibly have seen it before. But something within him was aware—the mysterious, fearful thing men called intuition—

He would *not* have left his niche. He would have done such nonsensical things as promoting the course he attempted; he would have spoken of his find to his friends and associates.

And he would have backed down whenever their ridicule endangered his association with them. He would have valued his place in the community his security or reputation—everything—above a full exploitation of intuition. He would have remained with New England; he would have remained a Statistical Man.

Something in him saw how it would be. And now he witnessed clearly on the lighted page of his mind the process of that seeing, the intricate course of its illogical flow.

The process that had made him once and for all a Non-Statistical Man.

It would be there again, he knew, doing its work out of sight of his living, reasoning awareness. He'd never doubt or mistrust it again. This was the very quality of faith he'd once suggested to Magruder!

"I wouldn't have left without being driven," he said slowly, his eyes still staring at the buildings on the other side of the street. "I'll never lose faith in my intuition again."

Magruder smiled a bit wistfully. "You'll need it; but you'll doubt the truth of your statement when intuition leads you through far hotter hells than anything you've seen up to now. And it will. Never doubt *that!*

"But, eventually, you will have a solid faith that can't be shaken by anything you encounter. You'll know by then that intuitive awareness excels crude logic in any basic crisis."

"It seems wrong," said Bascomb dubiously, "the way we've been talking and thinking about it. Like something outside myself, driving, directing and telling me what to do without any volition of my own. It gives me an uncomfortable feeling to think of it that way."

"IT SHOULD, because that's not the way to think of it. Intuition is not some mysterious, little green man in your skull, giving instructions and keeping back data from you.

"Intuition is *you*—a function of you, just as imagination, logic, or any other functions are. Like the subconscious, it does withhold data from the logic department at times; but that doesn't signify a separate entity by any means.

"The exact nature of intuition is, of course, still a mystery to us. We've only discovered how to restore it and use it to a degree. And like any other faculty, its operation can be improved and developed. What the top levels may be, we don't know; none of us has reached there, yet.

"You'll find there are some things intuition is not. Basically, it is a means of knowing things as they *do* exist, without particular recourse to the other senses, and relationships as they *are* and can be, without recourse to involved logic. Apart from this, it isn't a means of time travel to know everything that's going to occur in the future down to the end of your life. It *does* involve a considerable amount of prescience of the immediate future; but this fades exponentially as time increases the quantity of interlocking variables. It's one of our most valuable properties, however, and one which we're expanding rapidly.

"Basically, intuition seems to, function on the premise of direct contact with the universe. We have to postulate a condition of no distance, and simultaneous contact with all portions of the universe at once, or at least at will. It's very complex, but we think we're on the right track."

"I'll take your word for it," said Bascomb. "One thing I'd like to be able to understand, however, is the viciousness of the attacks on me back home. There was nothing normal about that; nothing I did could possibly explain it. The police ignored my requests for help, and vandals attacked my family at will. All because I defended an innocent man they wanted to kill!"

"No." Magruder shook his head. "Surely you don't believe the attack was result of your defense of Clementi?"

"What else?"

"That's one thing you *must* know, or one of the basic purposes of your coming has been lost. Look in your own mind and see if another reason is not apparent now."

BASCOMB considered and the illumination he'd experienced before seemed to burn slowly into brilliance again like a ripening sunburst. "Yes," he said, "I understand. Clementi had nothing to do with it. *They* thought Clementi was the reason; but actually they fought me because of what I'd tried to teach about intuition."

"That was it," said Magruder. "The fury of a statistical society breaking out at the appearance of its more desirable rival. You can't forget, surely, that men have always burned witches, and the few who found wisdom in their words. Prophets have always paid for their gift with their lives, in one way or another. Logic almost won; witches and prophets are few these days.

"You'll learn even more fully how dependence on Society inhibits a man's intuitive ability. You *have* learned that Society will fight Intuition, tooth and nail; it was absolutely necessary that you learn that lesson well."

"Why?" exclaimed Bascomb. "Wasn't the knowledge available intuitively, without going through this unpleasant experience?"

"DON'T MAKE the mistake of assuming intuitive replaces experience," Magruder said. "If that were true, we could become ascetics and spend our lives atop a high pole contemplating our belly buttons. Intuition serves to guide experience, not replace it. Intuitive knowledge that your neighbors would react as they did would not, of itself, have served to tear you from your statistical environment—without the actual experience of being subject to their reaction. It would have remained an academic matter, a further deterrent to your breaking away.

"Similarly, you might ask if people can detect their own need of insurance in advance, can they not change that need entirely. Can't they avoid accidents headed their way? Sometimes they can—if it is appropriate to their total optimum world-experience for them to do so. Other times they can only prepare to meet the experience in an optimum manner."

"But all your lecture students aren't going through what I did!"

"No—you're different because of what you are to become in this field. The others learn how to use it in their private lives, but they don't talk about it; their intuition teaches them how to keep out of such jams. Yours led you to it, because of the lesson you had to learn—because you had to know, first-hand, how your neighbors and friends could turn on you with cold, vicious savagery because of this thing.

"YOU HAD to see Society mobilizing all the witch burning techniques accumulated over the ages, and realize these still exist; that science has not made them unnecessary, but is sometimes only a milder form of the same thing. You had to know that Society recognizes your possession as a death warrant for itself that it will fight to the death for its own survival.

"You had to know how truly Man has become poor, little rich boy, sitting in the midst of his wealth of Christmas gadgetry, which has become abundant beyond his capacity to use it; and that inside, a slowly crumbling psyche is leaving him a hollow, eyeless shell, which will collapse upon the heap of that shining gadgetry when his last internal fires are dead.

"But I say logic *almost* won; the battle isn't quite over. Logic hasn't wholly dispelled the society of witches and prophets and sorcerers and soothsayers. Their company has been considerably augmented since our discovery of processes to restore intuitive faculties in spite of the social pressures against them.

"I started five years ago while still at the University. I recruited slowly and carefully, and all of my original people are still with me. We moved about the country later, working at random, developing our methods, improving our means of contact and sheer existence in a statistical society. You have encountered reports on some of our work, we are only beginning.

"SIX MONTHS ago, we decided on the experiment of taking over a whole community. We chose Myersville because it already had a good stable foundation; you know our results. It's to be our headquarters for some time to come.

"The general public here is not in on the secret of what, precisely, has happened to them, you understand. They are simply aware that they have decided to change their way of life; that they became fed up with the old one and voluntarily decided to improve. It shocks them now when they go away for a visit. But *we* didn't do this. They did—after having experienced release of some of their intuitive faculties, which led them to cease their slavish dependence on Society.

"That's about the whole story to date. We're trying to recruit stronger men as time goes on. Our survey of your abilities showed you to be one of the strongest."

"How could you know that?" Bascomb demanded abruptly. "I was buried, literally buried—in the statistical mass I called living. Why, Sarah's intuitive bullseyes scared the daylights out of me!"

"We knew that—and we knew why. Your inherent endowment of intuitive faculties is so high that you had to make a choice very early in life: bury them completely, or risk the terror of complete ostracism by the Society which would regard you as an enemy to its own existence.

"There's nothing shameful about that decision; it's the one the whole race made in the dawn of its life. It was particularly fortunate that you married a woman like Sarah, who already had some understanding and belief in her own intuitive powers. She will be a great help to us, also."

"You seem very sure we will go along with you!"

"Do you suppose we would have gone to the trouble we did, if we lacked positive, intuitive knowledge of that fact?" Magruder asked in astonishment.

Bascomb smiled in understanding. There was no argument to offer; he knew the Professor was quite correct. He knew it in the most positive way a man can ever gain any knowledge.

He *felt* it was the way things ought to be.

THE END

A WEAPON TO END ALL WARS...

The Martians were very concerned about Earth. They were worried that the destructive tendencies of their planetary neighbor might someday reach across the void and threaten the red planet itself. And now the Earthlings were on the brink of space travel with the development of a rocket ship in Nevada's high desert. It would be easier to simply eliminate the entire human race. A fast-acting worldwide virus would do the trick.

But there was one Martian who thought differently. He had faith in the human race, even if the Martian hierarchy did not. So the rulers of Mars gave humanity a final chance. And the fate of all Earthmen lay in the hands of two Martians who sped across the void in an ancient spacecraft toward Earth.

CAST OF CHARACTERS

FIS
All he wanted to do was save the human race. But to save it, he had to use one of the most terrible weapons ever invented.

DA
She was the most beautiful woman that anyone had ever laid eyes upon—and she wasn't even from Earth!

DAREN
As a middle-aged Martian (188 years old) he was much wiser than some of the young upstarts who wanted to save the Earth.

ANA
This aging Martian female had a bit of a sour disposition.   And she had no problem with the elimination of all Earthmen.

CHARLIE SMITH
He was the leader of "the Reds." And he led his army into battle armed only with flints and slingshots!

FORTESQUE
A war hero respected by all Englanders. Unfortunately his fame had perpetuated an arrogance that would cost him dearly.

MISSION FROM MARS

By
RICK CONROY

ARMCHAIR FICTION
PO Box 4369, Medford, Oregon   97501-0168

*For more information about Armchair Books and products, visit our
website at…*

www.armchairfiction.com

Or email us at…

armchairfiction@yahoo.com

CHAPTER ONE
Shall Earth Survive?

THE dome was the shape of an egg, and about seven hundred feet high. It glowed inside with a pale blue light, and being built of translucent material hung over Centralia, the capital city of the planet Mars, like a huge incandescent gem.

The egg-shaped dome was the home of Global Government in Mars. It hung above Centralia like a great, perceptive, benevolent brain.

Canals are the key to Martian prosperity. They not only irrigate the plants (rather like lichens), which the vegetarian Martians eat, but they also provide swift and cheap transport. Finally, the quantity of liquid flowing along one canal or another can be controlled, so as to control humidity and hence climate. No wonder the Martians are civilized. They have no weather to discuss, and so are obliged to converse on topics of greater social value.

The main task of the devoted workers in the Blue Brain was to control irrigation. Annual production of foodstuffs was planned to correspond exactly to population increases. Lichens were grown in the most favorable weather conditions, and swiftly transported to the main centers of population.

Police? Mars hasn't got any. Criminals (that is to say, those behaving in a way that annoyed their neighbors) were sent to Coventry. A criminal's own parents, wife and children would cooperate. And after a few days of total isolation—in which no one would speak to, feed, smile at or even glance at the offender—the criminal would be glad to apologize in public. The Martians have discovered how to create solitary confinement without going to the expense of constructing prisons.

But how do they know who is criminal? Is the transgressor branded, so that all will know to avoid him? Not so. The Martians have developed telepathy to a high pitch. Naturally some are more expert in reading the mind than others. And the least expert can tell right away the evil emanations that come from someone who is planning to defy law, and steal from, cheat, or hurt his neighbors. A man who turns criminal is said to "go bad," and his thought waves operate on the Martians just as a bad smell affects Earth dwellers.

Army?

The Martian children tell fairy stories among themselves of past legendary days when there were Martian armies and vast global wars. But these stories (which relate to a prehistoric time) are discouraged by the Martian adults as being liable to make the children "go bad."

Life on Mars could only survive if enough lichen for food were grown every year. Every time there was a war, people starved because the canals got blocked.

And so, because the Martians are much swifter at adapting themselves to new conditions than their cousins on Earth, a Global Government came into being. The mass of the Martians wanted it—and they have an advantage over Earth dwellers in being able to read the minds of their rulers, through telepathy. Propaganda cuts no ice on Mars.

The Martians can adapt themselves mentally with great speed to new situations—and for that, telepathy is mainly responsible. But their bodies also are adaptable.

Man could breathe on Mars only with the aid of special apparatus. He could walk only with the aid of machines to compensate for the difference in gravity. But the Martians can train to fit themselves for different conditions—extremes of heat and cold, more or less oxygen or other gases in the atmosphere, more or less gravity—in the same way as Earth dwellers trains themselves, for instance, to clip a fifth of a second off a hundred-meter record, or to swim the English Channel.

Three Martians walked around a narrow gallery on the outside of the Blue Brain, at its fattest part. Beneath them was a drop of four hundred feet. The gallery, despite the sheer drop, had no handrail. Martians are not made giddy by heights—the bony labyrinth of their inner ear is constructed differently from those of humans.

Daren's head was shaped rather like the Dome itself. His eyes—rather larger than those of Earth dwellers, and lacking in eyelashes—were blue, like the light that poured through the translucent walls of the building around which he walked. He was in late middle age—183 years old, the Martian year being about twice as long as the Earth year. He would soon be ready to retire.

"And before I go away from here," he was saying, "to do something simple like planting lichens, I want to get this business of Earth settled."

Fis, the young man beside him, smiled. He could tell that Daren's thoughts were not really of the simple life as a lichen planter. He had been fascinated by Earth for the last century. But it is good manners, among close friends on Mars, to talk instead of telepathizing, and not to make use of insight into the other's thoughts (unless, of course, there is danger of the other "going bad").

"Settled?" Fis asked.

The third figure, walking beside them, broke in sharply. Her voice was high-pitched—strident; Ana would have been a pleasanter companion if she had married years ago and had a family, instead of staying on her Level in the Blue Brain, worrying over Earth Problems.

"They're past all hope," she said. "Half an Earth century ago I still had some confidence in them. But since we installed the first telecinegraph that could project in color, they have gotten worse and worse. Remember when they started using poison gas on each other—taking advantage of their inability to adapt themselves quickly to new atmospheres? They'd been blowing each other to pieces for several centuries, of course—but about the same time it got very bad..."

"Worse was to come," said Daren, gloomily.

"You mean, destruction of each other by nuclear fission explosions—the so-called atom bomb? Yes, that's pretty bad. And now they've started on disease—spreading germs from the air, poisoning crops. I think they took a wrong turn some centuries back—"

"I don't agree—" the strong young voice of Fis broke in. He was leaning against the wall of the Blue Brain, gazing down on the illuminated city of Centralia spread out beneath him. His stomach wall adapted though it was to the horrors that came the way of a professional Earth-investigator—turned over sickly at the thought of someone dropping a bomb on his beloved Centralia—destroying places he remembered with affection, and people he loved.

"I don't agree," he repeated, in a confident voice, "that the Earth dwellers are past all hope. You look too much on the gloomy side. You must remember the disadvantages they work under. They can't read each other's thoughts. Half their time they spend in lying to each other and deceiving each other— they call it politics, or business, or journalism. Then they can't adapt themselves quickly. They are only beginning to tackle the diseases that enfeeble them—and then, not by living healthy lives, but by medicine. And they spend so much of their time trying to get enough food that it's not surprising they haven't yet got around to the much more important task of organizing a world government..."

"You're always making excuses for them," Ana broke in, sharply. "If you'd known them as long as I have, you'd be quite sick of them. They do things that are not merely confused, but quite insane. Like persecuting people who have a skin of a particular color or a nose of a particular shape..." Ana, whose skin was of a pale green shade, of which she was rather proud, had once been in danger of "going bad" by sneering at a girl downstairs in the Global Entertainment Department who had nice features, but a skin with purple blotches. Ever since then, she had taken pains to stress that she was against the color bar, both in Mars and on Earth.

"Concentration camps," said Daren, gloomily, "they were pretty bad. I couldn't sleep for a week after we picked up those pictures of Belsen on the telecinegraph."

"That's still no reason," said Fis, "for the Elected Global Brains to discuss ways and means of wiping out all Earth dwellers. It's so barbarous and filthy—to think of wantonly killing millions of creatures not unlike ourselves. Inferior, of course, and backward—near the level of animals, perhaps. But still people. And after all the research we've put into studying their habits and tabulating their peculiarities…"

Daren looked serious and glanced around him, as if making sure that no one was listening—either to his thoughts or words. "I've tried not to think about it," he said, his face stern, "ever since the Elected Global Brains drew me into the discussion. I didn't want the rumor to get around and distress the citizens of Centralia. But now I'm going to let my mind dwell on what they told me—just for a minute. And if you want to, you can Overthink me…"

The three stood there, in silence. Of course, both Ana and Fis were expert telepathists (or Over thinkers), or they would never have landed jobs in the Blue Brain. And as they picked up the thoughts that were passing through Daren's brain, their faces registered emotions. First—of bewildered incredulity. Then of disgust. Then of stern determination.

Just then a messenger from the Elected Global Brains Bureau appeared. "If you are Citizen Daren, from the Earth Research Enterprise, I've got an urgent message for you."

Daren nodded, reflecting that the Global Brains certainly picked all the prettiest messengers for their own department. But then, they deserved some compensation for the great responsibility they carried.

The messenger blushed prettily, as she Overthought the compliment Daren was thinking about her. Flirtation in Mars is a silent business. Perfect strangers, after a few moments' mutual Overthinking, find they have a great deal in common, and suddenly embrace, without passers-by being able to notice any preliminary signs of courtship.

The pretty messenger went on, "The Elected Global Brains are in session, and would like you to take your two chief assistants and be at the Bureau in eight minutes."

Daren nodded grumpily. He had Overthought her reaction to his compliment—that he was rather nice, and, of course, a very important man, but much too old to interest a pretty young girl with her life before her, and Global Brains themselves to flirt with.

There were ten Global Brains, seven male and three female. Every now and again the Martian females would start making a fuss about equal numbers of the sexes at the Bureau, but on Mars as on Earth the females preferred at the annual elections to vote for males rather than for their own sex.

They were all cheerful-looking persons—remarkably so, in view of their enormous responsibilities. They were the Trustees of the Martian Race. They thought ahead, warded off global dangers, tried to govern in the interests of the People of Mars. They were all highly expert Overthinkers, and each day spent a part of their time Overthinking the ordinary people, and finding out what they wanted. It was in this way—by telepathy—that Public Opinion had its effect in Mars. The Government listened in to the people, and did precisely what they wanted.

But Overthinking is somewhat fatiguing, even for the experts. So the Chairman of the Bureau spoke, "We have got the cooperation of the Medical Board in drawing up a plan for wiping out those two-legged, almost-Martian creatures that have multiplied in such numbers recently on Earth—"

Hearing his beloved Humans spoken of in these terms was too much for Fis. He burst out, youthfully, "I've been informed of your reason—but I don't think any reason is good enough for putting such a ghastly crime into effect!"

Eyebrows were raised at this word, crime. Most of the Board regarded their operation for wiping out Man as on a par with the slaughter on Earth of a number of animals who have caught hoof-and-mouth disease. Regrettable—but necessary.

"You know they are preparing, in the desert of—ah—" the chairman glanced at his notes, "Nevada, a rocket-launching site, the purpose of which is to send an expedition to Mars?"

Daren broke in and said, "I've done all the telecinegraph research on that myself, personally. But I thought it best to tell them, while we were on our way up here."

"What of that'?" said Fis. "It's a sign of progress. Five hundred Martian years ago, your predecessors, citizens, had a perfected rocket-apparatus for invading Earth. You remember the Mars-wide discussion that went on. You remember the decision that was taken in this very room—that we'd given Man a chance. He was in a pretty poor way then. The Dark ages were in full swing. Man was afraid of the dark. He went around hitting other men with clubs and stabbing them with spears—"

"And compared with that the atomic bomb," Ana murmured behind him, "is such an improvement..."

"Our forefathers gave him a chance," Fis retorted. "And I think it was a wise choice. Man has come a long way. He grows nearly enough food to nourish his race properly. It would be an improvement if he planned the growing of food on a global scale, as we do. But he may get that far yet. Thanks to his medical research he isn't so much at the mercy of disease..."

The Chairman of the Bureau seemed to he looking into space at some spot just over the young man's left shoulder. He liked his young men to be optimistic and confident. Mars would be in a poor way if the young got despondent. But meanwhile, his own time and that of the board was valuable. He rapped with his knuckle, and Fis, who heard the rapping sound and Overthought the unspoken criticism, stopped abruptly.

"Allowing these Earthmen to fly to Mars was a serious decision to take," he said. "We wanted all the evidence, before deciding. We put the director himself on to telecinegraph research on the rocket-launching site. He tells us that the rocket—a primitive and crude version of the one our forefathers developed five hundred years past—is nearly ready for use. Dare we let man on Mars? He has spiritual weaknesses—he can't Overthink, and he adapts himself poorly to new environments. But he carries with him infections. If he blows his own kind up with atomic bombs and spreads diseases deliberately among them, what will he do on Mars? There hasn't been a war on Mars since prehistoric times…"

"And is the threat so immediate?" Fis, in the dark about what was happening in Nevada (the American continent was Daren's special sector) made his last plea.

The Chairman folded his hands, smiled.

"Immediate? Two or three Earth years. When war breaks out on Earth between the two rival power-blocs, the winners will conquer the Earth. That will only take perhaps two or three years, given these new—what do you call them—what's the old expression?"

"Weapons—" prompted a member of the Board, who had once been a professor of ancient history.

"And then what is there for them to conquer—except Mars? We must stop them now—"

Daren said, "And how, citizen, do you propose—"

The Chairman smiled broadly and said, "This young man won't remember the outbreak of our last serious epidemic—the shivering fever. That was before we eliminated dangerous bacteria on Mars. But the bacteriology section of the Department of Public Health has kept cultures of this bacteria, with due precautions, for scientific reasons. It's a bacteria that doesn't occur on Earth. Men will die like flies when it begins to spread—you remember the shivering fever, Daren, even Martians found it hard to cope with?"

"But you'll simply wipe them out," Fis protested.

"They are busy wiping themselves out. We shall merely accelerate the process."

"But you'll destroy a whole species," said Fis, with all the passion of a scientist.

"How many species has man himself destroyed?" asked the Chairman, calmly. "Why do you think Man is more worth saving than the Dodo, a stupid bird, which he killed until it became extinct?"

Just then the prettiest messenger by far of the Elected Global Brains Bureau came tripping into the conference room. The Global Brains were used to pretty messengers, and equally used to controlling their thoughts. Daren was a Martian in late middle age; Ana was a sour old spinster. So it couldn't, by a sheer process of elimination, have been their unspoken thoughts which caused the messenger to blush a delicate shade of pink.

Fis noted that she, like himself, had the coloring of a dominant tribe on Earth—a sort of whitish pink. A quite unusual coloring on Mars, and one which accounted for the color of her blush. Ana, for instance, on the rare occasions when she felt obliged to blush, went a deep olive-green. He tried to Overthink to the messenger a suggestion that she should hang around outside until the meeting was over, so they could get to know each other better. But she was busy Overthinking something complimentary about his broad shoulders, and so the wires got crossed. It's very confusing if two Martians Overthink at the same time.

The Chairman took the message she had brought, looked at it thoughtfully, then dropped it on the table.

"This argument, citizens, is already made a little futile."

"The war on Earth—?" guessed Ana.

"The war on Earth started at midnight."

"It will have to be shivering fever, I'm afraid," said a member of the Board. But he said it kindly, because the young man's enthusiasm for his work had impressed him.

The kind note prompted Fis to make one last attempt; "You won't give them a chance? You won't think of some other way? They're a frightfully interesting species, really. Admittedly, there are a few of them who act like madmen, but there are a number of fine fellows among them—women who bring up families in poverty—"

"Poverty?" asked a member of the Board, questioningly.

"An Earth term," explained Fis, "meaning, not enough to eat."

"Of course, it's unplanned down there, isn't it?" the Global Brain murmured.

The Chairman was once more rapping the table. "I'm only Chairman of the Elected Global Brains," he remarked, ironically, "and among us we can't think of a better plan. But Mars is a democracy, and this wouldn't be the first time that some member of the rank and file has done better than the rest of us put together. I give you until this time tomorrow, young man, to save your pets. If you can think of a good scheme to overcome the danger facing Mars, we'll try it. But it will have to be good."

Outside in the corridor, Fis noted that the pink-and-white messenger was hanging about, pretending to be lacing her shoe.

"See you in a moment," thought Fis.

Ana, who was last through the door, said, "You've certainly landed yourself a job, young Fis." But Daren, who had Overthought the young man's reaction to the presence of the waiting messenger, and who had been young himself once, took Ana firmly by the hand and led her away. Looking back over his shoulder he winked at his colleague, a large lid without eyelashes sliding back and forth across an even larger eye.

"I've got the rest of the day off," the messenger girl said. The fact that she spoke told Fis that she had made up her mind this wasn't to be just a brief emotional relationship—a few minutes' mad Overthinking, and then an embrace. She wanted to take it easy, find out all about him first.

"Then let's go," he answered. The survival of two thousand millions of the human race depending on his solving the problem which the Chairman had given him. How to stop the war on Earth. And here he was, wasting time on romance.

"Then let's go," he said, a second time, taking her arm and Overthinking a compliment about the way she had done her hair.

Alcohol has no effect on the Martians—they use it as a chemical, distilling it from lichen by-products. If anyone suggested drinking it, they'd think he was crazy. If they want to intoxicate themselves, they sniff a Quintessential Box.

The Quintessential Box was invented near the end of the period on Mars that had been marked by the petering out of war. The name of the benefactor to the Martian race is lost in antiquity, but even the resources of modern Martian science have been able to make very little improvement on his original pattern.

The Quintessential Box is shaped a little like an Earthly gas mask (civilian pattern), with the earpieces removed. Nose and mouth are thrust into the face-piece, and the addict inhales from the box.

There's nothing in the box that causes a smell to develop. There may be a dozen people in the room, each smelling different odors from attar of roses to creosote, and still the room itself will not contain an odor. The Quintessential Box contains a radio circuit, which stimulates by micro-radiation those cells of the brain where the memory of scents is stored. So the better developed the imagination, and the richer the experience of different perfumes, the more intoxicating the use of the box can be.

Fis, and the messenger girl, called Da, sat on a promontory overlooking the Grand Martian Canal (which in that part of Centralia is used for pleasure boats). They had one thing in common, anyway—they were both Quintessential Box addicts, and very expert at their use.

They were both taking deep breaths, with their faces wreathed in smiles.

Da lifted her head. "New-mown lichen," she said.

"A bit hackneyed," he teased. "I was smelling wet lamb's wool."

She ducked her head again. Then lifted it. "Spring water," she said.

"Onions," he answered, teasing.

"A garden full of sweet peas, on a hot day."

"Hot dinner," he said, "after a day's winter sports at the Pole." (The Poles, North and South, are the favorite playgrounds on Mars. The South Pole is slightly more fashionable, because the Aurora there is somewhat more spectacular than at the North Pole.)

"Canal liquid," she said, "on a summer evening—" And that was as near as any personable young man on whatever planet could need to an invitation to a trip on a gondola.

The gondolas were made of iron, controlled magnetically. The specific gravity of the liquid was so great that the canal had something of the consistency of a comfortable rubber mattress, on which it was possible for a swimmer to float for hours without effort. The iron gondolas floated on the liquid as light as feathers.

They lay close to each other, letting the gondola drift in the magnetic streams laid down automatically, so that collisions were impossible, and effort, unnecessary.

"Tell me about your family," he began. And with most girls that would have been the prelude to a nice cozy chat.

But Fis Overthought a great wave of panic from the girl. "You don't have to tell me," he said, "if you don't want to…"

"I suppose it is time I got over it," she said. "But I found the disgrace so hard to bear. In fact, one of the Elected Global Brains—the little bald fellow, on the extreme left this morning—Overthought the fact that I was distressed when he passed me in the street one morning, and got me my job in the Bureau to restore my self-confidence—"

"I hope that was his only motive," said Fis, who had noticed that the bald-headed brain possessed a roving eye.

"Oh, yes—he was one of the few who knew about the disgrace—"

"Well?" Fis was by now deeply intrigued.

"The fact is, my father went bad," she said the last two words with abject horror.

Fis knew that "going bad" was a dying phenomenon on Mars. Practically only the mentally unbalanced thought that the proceeds of a crime were worth the penalty of being ignored by everyone else in the community.

"Did he steal something?"

She shook her head vigorously, as if such a petty crime were totally unworthy of the family honor.

"He's all right in the head, I suppose?"

"Of course."

"Not—oh, I say. Not murder, or something like that—"

She compressed her lips, and shook her head.

"Worse," she said. She looked from one side to the other. Except for a middle-aged female of ample dimensions in a bathing dress who was lounging on the canal liquid taking deep breaths from her Quintessential Box, there was no one near. And by the look on the fat woman's face, she was so busy dreaming up the smells from five-course meals that she would neither overhear or even Overthink.

"He was an inventor. And he invented—" her voice went almost inaudible with horror, "he invented a *weapon.*"

The average Martian would have been deeply shocked. But Fis had spent his five-hour working day for some years glued to his telecinegraph, watching the antics of humans on Earth. He was used to these antique barbarities.

"Not a gun?" he asked. "Not a bombing airplane?"

"I don't know what those things are," she said, "though they sound dreadful. No—my father had been apprenticed to one of the men who built the Space Rocket they've got up at the museum—the one they've never used. The man always thought the decision to scrap it had been wrong, and he brought up my father to believe so. He put into his mind a number of weird old ideas—like ambition, and greed and lust for power—you know, the things they used to tell us about in fairy stories—"

"Oh—hate and jealousy and all that kid stuff—" Fis said.

"So father set himself to invent—what I said. He was very clever about it, really. He was a metallurgist, and very fond of music. In the evenings, when he came in from his laboratory, he would play on the oshlak." (The oshlak is a Martian stringed instrument played with a bow.)

The girl's voice had a haunted quality that gripped Fis' mind.

"There was a crystal drinking vessel on the table, and at one point in the scale he was playing it started to shake and quiver—" The girl did a little quiver of her own for good measure, and Fis comfortingly tucked his arm tighter around her. "He had found its—something or other—"

"Harmonic frequency," said Fis, a trifle absently. He was finding it difficult to admire Da's profile and listen to her story at the same time.

"And he kept bowing the same note, and making the glass shake more and more, until it shivered into tiny splinters. It sort of…exploded. It was incredible—"

"It's an old trick at parties," said Fis, "though as a rule only a professional oshlak player can bow accurately enough."

"But you didn't see the expression on his face!" she protested. "It was horrible—evil. If we had known our duty, my mother and I, we would have known from that moment that he had gone bad, and cut him off ourselves. But he vanished into his laboratory, and stayed there for days. We used to push food through the door to him. And then he came out, with a small box, and went to see one of the Elected Global Brains. My father was a well known inventor, even celebrated, and had no difficulty in gaining access to him. And what passed between them I don't exactly know. But the upshot was that everyone concluded not only that father had gone bad, but that he was a more extreme case than anyone else had ever been for years. Father was so afraid, when the awful thing he had done began to dawn on him, that he simply disappeared."

"Anyone," said Fis, sympathetically, "whose father had gone bad would feel distressed about it. But why, if he'd invented a weapon, did he take it to a Global Brain?"

And then a sudden burst of inspiration broke over him. He only half-heard the first words of Da's reply. Then realized that everything she said was of first-rate importance. Might actually save those poor pitiful creatures on Earth from being wiped out by shivering fever. "...suggested to the Global Brain that he could dominate all the other brains with this weapon. Have his own way. Power—that was the thing he was supposed to be tempted by. Although if a Global Brain was likely to be tempted by power, who on Mars would be mad enough to elect him? My father tried to tell the Brain that with this weapon he could force everyone to obey him. Flirt with all the most beautiful women. Have people fear him. All the old fairy story things..."

"Atavism," Fis murmured. But already he was fiddling with the electro-magnetic device on the prow of the gondola, so that it headed toward shore. "We've got to go and see the Chairman of the Elected Global Brains—right away."

Then he Overthought that she was reflecting what an important man he must be, though so young (barely 50) if he went racing off to the Chairman at the slightest thing. And she Overthought that he wasn't even flattered at the reflection. So, to cause him to respect her more, she said, "Atavism? What is that?"

He whistled down an Anti-gravitational Self-guided Cabriolet. They took their seats. He slid into section the sheets of anti-gravitational alloy, so that the Cabriolet rose in the air. Then he rotated it so that it pointed toward the Blue Brain, and homed toward the Cabriolet Rank at the top of the egg.

"Atavism? They get it on Earth. It means a reversion to primitive type. Quite often there, after a hundred years or so of behaving themselves, they go back to the animal stage. Take torture, for instance. That means, causing the nerves deliberate distress, often by mechanical means." The girl shivered at the mere thought. "But they soon get rid of it and decide never to use it again. And then, hey presto! Some atavism occurs among a backward section, and they are all busy torturing each other again. What's more, they revel in scenes of torture. They project it over the very primitive telecinegraph they've got on Earth, called films, and even let children see it happening."

Her face was absolutely white, and for a moment he regretted telling her. It was hard for someone like himself, who viewed the Earth-antics from a scientific point of view, to realize its effects on other Martians.

Finally she regained control. In a tight, restrained little voice, she said, "I certainly hope you don't for a moment imagine my father did anything quite so dreadful."

"Nothing of the sort," he said. "Atavisms up here can't be so bad, of course. But evidently they can occur—though it's the first one I've ever heard tell of."

At the Bureau a handsome male clerk nodded in far too amiable a way at Da. But when Fis gave his name, the clerk showed much more respect. "The Chairman left your name out here," he said, "and Overthought us that you were to be let in right away if you turned up."

"Thank you, citizen," said Fis, coldly, "and Citizeness Da will see him, too."

And Da's particularly pretty nose went at least a quarter of an inch higher in the air.

"It's brave of you, Citizeness," said the Chairman, "to be willing to have this old scandal dragged up for the sake of some poor demented creatures on another planet." Though, even as he spoke, he could Overthink that her motive was actually a sane, young and particularly attractive male creature on the planet Mars.

"Yes, there was a weapon. I know where it is, and I know what it will do. But it will take a vote of the entire Bureau to get it into your hands. At the time it was invented, the Bureau wondered whether to destroy it or not. The view prevailed that such a power should be in the hands of the Trustees, in case another atavism occurred that couldn't be handled easily. I didn't think it was an especially good decision. All the time the weapon exists on Mars, it will constitute what our forefathers used to call a temptation. Personally, I'd support any move to take it right away to another planet and use it for a sensible scientific purpose…"

"And how soon," asked Fis, "can the Board arrange to meet?"

The Chairman of the Elected Global Brains smiled and said, "Although we Brains are the only people on Mars who work an eighteen-hour day, we can't arrange to come together instantaneously for your benefit, young man—"

Fis looked embarrassed, and mumbled something about the preservation of the Man species being essential to Science.

"If you hadn't got some good reason like that, we shouldn't be taking chances with these dangerous little monsters on Earth. Tell you what I'll do. I think this is a big enough emergency to warrant the use of the Mechanical Overthinker—"

Fis and Da both drew in their breath with excitement. The Mechanical Overthinker was one of the most celebrated inventions that the Brains had at their personal disposal—they had the only specimen on Mars. It boosted the power of individual thought so that it could be transmitted over distances—but since it seriously interfered with private thoughts, it was only used rarely. There is on Mars a high degree of respect for the thoughts of the individual.

"Can I see it working, sir?" asked Fis.

But the Chairman was peremptory. "It gives anyone near it a headache. That's why we don't use it very often. I'll get my headache for your sake, calling the Board together. One is straightening out a blockage of canal traffic down on the Equator. Two of the Female Brains are studying next year's plan for building Maternity Homes. And the Brain who got you your job, young lady, has gone to the Electro-Magnetic Ballet—it's his day off. Now while I'm giving myself a headache on the Mechanical Overthinker, you had better go upstairs and check on the progress of this silly childish what-you-may-call-'um—this war—on Earth. Then go down to the Medical Board and arrange to be conditioned to Earth atmosphere, temperature, and pressure. That antiquated rocket in the museum takes two—if you're going to use it, as I Overthink you are, you'd better choose a companion..."

Da suddenly realized that both the men had Overthought what was passing through her mind. She blushed scarlet.

"I should hesitate before asking to go," said the Chairman, "they're pretty beastly to females on Earth—isn't that so, Fis?"

"It varies," Fis mumbled. He didn't like to be caught out like that—but the attitude of Earth inhabitants to their females was one of the things about them he found hardest to defend. He had once had a party of friends in to watch an Earth "film" on a telecinegraph, as a novelty.

But they had been able to see two things that shocked them profoundly. A moving picture of an Earth male hitting—yes, actually *hitting*—an Earth female. And also, the fact that the hall where the "film" was shown was full of children. It had taken Fis months to live down his profound emotion of shame on his pets' behalf.

"I don't care," she said. "I'll—take the chance—it's in the cause of science. And besides, I want to dedicate this act to my father. He's gone bad, but if I dedicate this to him, he may think about it and go good again."

Criminals who are "shut out" on Mars have the chance of release if someone is willing to dedicate a good act to them. They reflect on that good act, particularly if it is difficult or dangerous, and the fact that someone is prepared to do such a thing with them in mind often stops those who have gone bad from going worse. In fact, often they go good.

"And you, Fis?" asked the Chairman.

"I'll be glad to have her," said Fis, "and I sincerely hope that if ever I have the misfortune to go bad, someone will think enough of me to dedicate such a dangerous act to me.

The telecinegraph is one of the triumphs of Martian science.

As the Martians look up into their night sky, they can see the other stars and planets. Venus, of course, looking very bright, and Earth shining gloriously with her single moon. The light that comes from Earth is the rays of the sun reflected from the surface of the Earth. If analyzed those light-waves would be found to contain visual evidence of everything happening on Earth—because the light of the sun is reflected from every activity on the face of the globe.

The first telecinegraph was developed to pick up and analyze the sun's light-waves reflected by the Earth and transmitted direct to Mars. Of course, the image was very feeble, and the whole device took a great deal of controlling. But then a great improvement was made by the invention of the *historical* telecinegraph, or H.T. for short. This picked up not just the light waves transmitted direct from Earth to Mars, but also those radiating in every direction through space. Events that had happened millions of years ago on Earth were still contained in the light traveling eternally through space. The whole history of the Earth since the continents were formed was thereafter permanently on tap in the Earth Research Enterprise laboratories in the Blue Brain.

The laboratory where Ana worked was dark, except for a glow from the screen of the telecinegraph.

"Close your eyes!" she said, sharply, when she noticed that Fis had a girl and a stranger with him. Obediently Da shut her eyes. Ana went on, "Don't open them until I say. Now, listen. What you are going to see is very horrible. The Earth dwellers have started their beastly war, and it's horrible even to scientists like us who have years of experience in dealing with them. Make a great effort to control yourself. Now—think carefully. Do you want to open your eyes?"

"Yes," said Da, firmly.

"Brave girl," Fis murmured.

Because it was pretty ghastly. When doing his research into the Decay of Earth Civilization in the Twentieth Century—three years ago—Fis had seen most of the bloodier battles. Ypres and the Somme. The Dardanelles, Stalingrad, Burma and the Falaise Gap. Bodies of men blown to pieces. Horrible sights and sounds. But this was worse.

A faint sob from Da beside him made him realize that she was finding this horror—a bombing raid in the Orient—rather hard to bear.

"Beasts," she was whispering. "They must all be like beasts…"

Ana Overthought Fis' suggestion that she should move the viewer a little away from the front line. She touched a knob and a new scene came up clear. Two soldiers of one army, separated from their unit, were walking wearily along a road. From the wreckage around, bombers had recently passed that way.

From a ruined hut at the roadside evidently came sounds, because the soldiers turned to face that way. One was wounded—his wound in the arm could be seen as he turned.

The unwounded one went to the ruined hut, pushed back a wooden beam that had tumbled across the doorway. Through the doorway stumbled a woman, holding a child in her arms.

From her Oriental features it was plain to see that she was of a different race—as Earth dwellers call it—from the two soldiers.

The unwounded soldier—coal-black—took the child in his hands.

"Is he—he's not—surely he's not going to *kill* it!" whispered Da, aghast.

"They're not that bad," Ana grumbled, sourly. "I've seen happenings like this several times. And I daresay Fis has seen dozens of them when he was doing his research into the Decay of Civilization. They can behave quite like Martians sometimes. Yet they never seem to apply it—"

"Look!" Da interrupted, delighted. The black soldier was giving the Oriental child some sort of delicious food. The Oriental woman—mother of the child—was binding up the wound in the arm of the pink-white soldier. "I see what you mean," said Da, softly. "They *are* worth saving. They *will* make something of themselves some day."

Ana turned. "You young people," she said, tartly, "Incorrigible optimists…"

CHAPTER TWO
Rocket Honeymoon

"EARTH CONDITIONING is pretty tough," said Fis. "D'you think you can stand it?"

Da smiled. "It won't make my hair drop out, or something like that?"

"No, you'll be even more beautiful when you've been scientifically conditioned to stand a pressure of fifteen pounds per square inch."

And they stepped through the doorway into the Conditioning Room.

"Haven't conditioned anybody for Earth," said the operative, "since the time my father before me had this job, and there was talk of sending a rocket to Earth. I've been looking over the old documents this morning—they did a lot of work on it in those days. It's a straightforward job. Atmosphere of oxygen, nitrogen, carbon dioxide and water vapor, with a few unimportant inert gases. Take this pill—that will do the trick. No—don't take it now, Miss. Later on, when you're approaching an Earth atmosphere—for goodness sake read the instructions on the label. Pressure, I'm afraid, you'll have to go into the chamber for. You'll find that the so-called low temperatures on Earth are child's play to a Martian, but my father recommends here in his notes a little conditioning against high temperatures. Anything else?"

"Languages?" asked Da.

"I speak the main Earth languages," Fis said, "English, Russian, Chinese and Spanish. And a smattering of Urdu and Arabic."

"So they are thinking of sending a rocket over, after all," said the operative. "I imagined it must be something like that."

"It's hush-hush," Da said. "Don't even let yourself be Overthought about it."

"That will take rather an effort," said the operative. "I'm not exactly a Global Brain. And we're not used to secrets on Mars. Anyway, I hope they give you a better spaceship than that old crock in the Centralia Museum of Antiquities…"

Old crock was right.

Standing there, Da's hand linked loosely with his own, Fis looked up at the metallic monster—kept bright daily by the Museum charwoman with her Vacuum Blow-lamp.

It brought back to him memories of his boyhood. He had already decided to be a scientist, and had romantic ideas a bout the possibilities of Space Travel. He had stood, a small boy, in the Museum of Antiquities, looking up at the Rocket and reflecting sadly that it was destined never to be used.

He had even felt resentment against the decision of the Elected Global Brain not to send it. Though such resentment might have had a bad outcome—look how it had affected Da's father.

And then, later on, in his work at the Earth Research Enterprise, he had several times thought how wise a decision it had been to let these Earth creatures work out their own destiny. They had made mistakes, but there had been a lot of progress.

"So that's the Space Ship," said Da, at last.

"Nice for a honeymoon," said Fis, jokingly.

"We shan't have time on the way over," she answered, sternly, "for anything except learning languages…"

The Space Rocket was quite ingenious. It worked partly on a rocket principle, partly by a device like those that operated the Anti-gravitational Self-guided Cabriolet.

"Briefly," Fis explained, "the principle is this. Here are the sheets of anti-gravitational alloy. You pull them into section—

no, don't touch, you'll send us shooting through the roof of the Museum of Antiquities. There's the radar apparatus—we home in on Earth in the same way that we might home in on the Blue Brain when returning from a gondola trip. The sheets, being in section, cut off the influence of the gravity of Mars. We shoot up through the atmosphere until the pull of gravity from Mars is weakened. Then the rocket apparatus comes into play—"

"If it doesn't?"

"If it doesn't we just go flying at random through space. So it had better. That's a risk we take. Then when we come into the influence of the Earth's gravitational field the rocket apparatus shuts off, and we control our descent by putting just enough sheets of the alloy into section to reduce the influence of gravity."

"I can bring an ordinary Cabriolet down without the slightest bump," she said.

"Then you'd better be the one who brings the rocket down gently," he suggested.

"Oh, no," she answered. "You're a male. I'm leaving the mechanical side of things to you. And, besides, I'll be too busy learning languages."

"And they wonder," said Fis to the world at large, "why they only elect three females out of ten to the Elected Global Brains…"

Fis supervised bringing out the rocket. It was erected on a plain outside Centralia—flying there gently under the influence of its own anti-gravitational sections.

The Warden of the Plain-which was used normally for Martian sports—said churlishly, "You'll have to move that thing off there by tomorrow. There's a Hemisphere Sports Semi-final in the afternoon."

"Maybe," said Fis, "our departure will be an added attraction…"

When Fis and Da returned to the Blue Brain, nine of the ten Brains had already returned, and were gravely discussing Da's father's "weapon."

The missing one was the man with the roving eye.

"We've got a quorum, it's all right," said the Chairman. But just then the tenth Brain arrived, looking rather disheveled.

"Sorry I'm late," he mumbled, "but as it was my day off I went to the ballet. They've got a wonderful orange colored ballerina, just moved to Centralia from the Grand Junction Canal district. Her technique is superb…"

The Chairman rapped the table, then brought from beneath it a small box.

Da stuffed her tiny fist in her pretty mouth, and bit hard on her knuckles.

"That's the box—that's the thing that father brought here that morning…"

"Now, now, my dear. Calm yourself," said the Brain with the roving eye, who had arrived late.

The Chairman was opening the box gingerly, and taking out an object like a "pistol" (a sort of "weapon" used on Earth), with a barrel an inch and a quarter in diameter, and a square chamber above the grip.

"A first-rate brain was wasted when the man who invented this went bad," he said. "But fortunately there's always a bright side. I think this pistol may hold the key to the problem of Earth…"

"But what does it *do?*" asked one of the female Brains.

"I shall have to be careful with it," said the Chairman, walking across to the translucent wall and removing a section. Through the opening the Brains could see the open sky and in the distance the lovely Martian countryside on the outskirts of Centralia.

The Chairman Overthought, and promptly a messenger entered carrying a metal pot about a foot high. The Chairman put it on the ledge made by the removed section. On her way out, the messenger spared an admiring glance for Da, her former colleague, sitting among these celebrities as if she had been born to do so.

"Look," said the Chairman. "I've carefully studied the instructions for using this. The knob here can be turned to alter the range of this pistol. It can let out a—let us call it, a vibrating ray—fifty miles wide and five hundred long. Or, alternatively, a narrow ray three inches wide and ten feet long. Or anything of intermediate size. I'll turn this control to the minimum, to prevent accidental damage to Cabriolets flying near the Blue Brain. Now watch—"

He pressed the trigged of the ray gun. There was a faint crackle and something like a spark appeared to flash at the muzzle.

Then they looked at the metal pot.

Or rather, they looked where it had been.

A faint circle of brown dust ringed the ledge.

"Goodness," said one of the Brains, "I do hope you haven't knocked it off the ledge. It might hurt someone on the balcony beneath."

The Chairman gently shook his head.

"Nothing like that."

"You mean—it has just disappeared?"

"Its molecular structure has been radically transformed. In brief, it isn't metal, any more. It's just dust. And this works on all the common metals. Here's a laboratory report that was made when it was turned over to the Global Brains for safekeeping. It simply disintegrates metal—doesn't need any charging. Now just imagine. Think how necessary metal is even on Mars, where we have developed so many synthetic substances. For instance, in the foundations of the Blue Brain there are some struts of beryllium bronze, in a place where we wanted a strong non-ferrous alloy. A couple of seconds' work with this pistol accurately aimed and the Blue Brain itself would tumble."

Ii didn't need much imagination to realize the possibilities inherent in such a weapon. With it, one person could withstand an army. If everything made of metal disintegrated, nothing would be left of a rifle except the wooden butt. Nothing would be left of a tank except the rubber seating, and a dirty splash of oil on the road. Yet not a man would be harmed, except, of course, the unfortunate pilots of bombing planes, or troops that happened just at that moment to be marching over metal bridges.

"Now the question," said the Chairman, "is whether Citizen Fis here is to be trusted with this weapon. I personally recommend that he should be. I admire the stand he is making for the preservation of this species on Earth. I like to see our young men prepared to make personal sacrifices for the sake of Science."

"Agreed," "Agreed," rattled all around the table, until it came to the last man—the professor of ancient history. He looked as though he was going to make an objection. Then, finally, unwillingly, he said, "Agreed—on one proviso—"

"Which is?"

"I don't trust these evil-minded creatures on Earth. I agree that Fis and his companion should go, and should take the weapon. But I think we should right away start manufacturing new Space Rockets, and stocking up the bacteria of shivering fever. I think his journey should be checked the whole time by telecinegraph. And the moment it looks like his mission is failing, or the Earth creatures seize this gun—and there's a danger they may—and then, heaven forbid, set out for Mars..." He waved his hand eloquently, and left the sentence unfinished.

"Very sensible precaution," said the Chairman.

"I insist also," said the history professor finally, "that their first act on landing should be to destroy the rocket in which they traveled. We don't want Earth diseases and atom bombs up here. And the Earth creatures are imitative enough—like monkeys—to be able to work the rocket."

The room grew tense. They could see the professor's point of view—even Fis and Da, condemned to exile among the sub-

Martian humans with their wars and color-bars, could see that he was right.

They couldn't take chances. They couldn't afford to have Mars invaded by a species that tortured and murdered each other, and suffered from ancient diseases like fear, hate, and lust for power.

"How do you fancy," asked Fis of Da, trying to make light of it, "being a martyr for the sake of science?"

"I've dedicated this act to my father," she, simply. "Maybe when he hears, it will cause him to become a good citizen again."

"No need to get too despondent," said the Chairman, as cheerfully as he knew how, "we shall be following you all the time on telecinegraph. There's just a chance we shall be able to send out an expedition and bring you home."

But of course, that sort of hearty reassurance doesn't go down so well on Mars, where people can reach each other's thoughts. Fis and Da knew they were virtually doomed. They looked into each other's eyes and Overthought madly for a few moments. The Global Brains had too much delicacy to Overthink what was passing through the two young people's minds. Let them make their own decision.

Finally Fis turned, and spoke for both of them, "We'll go," he said.

It's very difficult to keep a secret on Mars. People let their minds dwell on the secret, and before they know where they are, someone has Overthought them. It means there's singularly little hypocrisy, but it makes the job of the Global Brains much harder, because they have to spend their time avoiding thinking of things that it would be better for their people not to know.

Whether the operator at the Conditioning Chamber, or the Warden out at the Sports-plain had allowed his knowledge of the trip to be Overthought, or whether some messenger girl in the Blue Brain had been indiscreet, we shall never know. The fact is that by the time the rocket had been hauled on to its launching stand, the plain was filled with half the population of Centralia. A Martian can never resist a good show. They got the biggest gate that year at the Hemisphere Semi-finals that they'd had in two centuries.

Fis had let Da go home and pack a few things. Meanwhile, he was having a last check over the apparatus.

Yes, that rocket was really a museum piece.

The Museum was sealed against corrosion, of course, for the sake of its contents, but five hundred years is still five hundred years. The anti-gravitational sections were deuced stiff—no one had thought of lubricating the bearings with graphite, as they should be every half-century.

Fis made sure that fresh liquid oxygen was put in the rocket's fuel chamber. He had mastered the quite-simple rocket-firing device, but of course there was no opportunity of practicing with it. That was a chance they would have to take, once they got outside their planet's gravitational pull.

They loaded large stores of food and drink. One could only guess what the food would be like on Earth—the usual chemical combinations, of course, like proteins and fats. But what tastes?

Then, as a last concession to sentiment, Fis put on board the Quintessential Boxes, with which Da and he had intoxicated themselves in the iron gondola. Something to remember that by. They would help while away on the voyage. And besides, by the look of Earth battlefields, they would smell pretty vilely of carrion. A Quintessential Box might be a lifesaver.

Fis was having a last check over the controls, when a roaring sound from outside the rocket hatch prompted him to poke his head out.

The amphitheater around the Centralia stadium was crammed with faces, like a living rainbow. Faces of every color under the sun, orange, purple, green, and even a few pink-white faces like those to be found in such numbers on Earth. And they were roaring their applause, pressing in the direction of the entrance.

The crowd around the entrance was such that no one could move. Then, eventually, under the instructions of the Warden, everyone eased back and let through the person who was the center of attention.

They were carrying her shoulder-high. Her long, fine Martian hair had become loosened in the excitement, and was flowing in the wind.

The news had got around that this girl was voluntarily making the rocket trip to Earth, to save a scientific species. And that she was dedicating the trip to her father, who had gone bad years before. Now that would have been impressive, even if the "girl" had been some withered old spinster of a couple of hundred or so. But so far from being a withered crone, she was actually a stunning beauty.

And so Mars had what it enjoys—a heroine.

But since on Mars a heroine is able to Overthink the frank admiration of the men who surround her, it is liable to turn her head.

When Fis looked out of the rocket hatch, there was a mild, but a very mild, cheer from the section of the crowd nearest him, which anyway was so excited it would have cheered anything or anyone. He Overthought the wild reaction of the heroine-worshipping mob: "That man with the graphite stain on his face must be the mechanic."

The mechanic! He, Fis, the young white hope of the Earth Research Enterprise. The Martian who had been entrusted by the Global Brains with the Metal Annihilating Ray.

He looked at the box containing the pistol, and then at the metal stands, crammed around the rim of the Stadium by cheering Martians. He thought of the sensation that would be created if those stands turned to dust...

Then he clenched his fists. Such wicked, absurd thoughts— of jealousy and revenge. This is what came of watching Mankind—one became less than Martian as a result.

She came into the rocket with the air of an empress. Faces crowded around the hatch, peering in on her, as she sat in one of the two seats and began coquettishly pinning up her hair, pretending not to notice her audience.

Maliciously, Fis said, "Stand back from that hatch—it's dangerous." And the faces disappeared as if by magic.

"Watching me—dangerous?" she asked, with a dazzling smile, having Overthought his real motive for scaring the admirers away.

"Don't mind what I say," he said, a little enviously, "I'm just the mechanic."

She rose, came over toward him, patted his cheek. Since Overthinking the frank admiration of the Martians roaring cheers across the stadium, she had acquired a great deal more poise.

"So he wanted to make a speech, all about science, when we departed. And that silly girl he was so misguided as to take with him made a peepshow of herself..."

"Sit down in that chair," he said, sharply. "And see if you can at least buckle on your safety belt properly. We start, according to my calculations, in four minutes thirty-eight seconds exactly."

"But aren't you going to strap yourself in?"

"I can't be both strapped in and work the alloy sections," he said. "That's a bad fault in the design..."

He went over to the control panel, portable chronometer in one hand, and a sheet of calculations in the other.

His eyes were fixed on the moving arm of the chronometer, as it trembled jerkily toward the mark.

With one second to go, he put out his hand toward the handle operating the first section. The rest were connected in parallel, and would automatically slide themselves in after the first impulse was manually given.

As his hand closed over the handle, and moved, he thought he heard a roaring sound. It might have been the cheering of the crowd, penetrating even the alloy and plastic structure of the rocket. Then his mind whirled around and went first blazing red and then black.

He awoke with an excruciating headache, which was relieved by something exquisitely soft and gentle being passed tenderly across his forehead.

Something dazzling was close to his eyes. He felt like a child again, recovering from a serious illness, and being gently attended by his mother.

The gentle touch was of Da's hand. The dazzling object was her face, so beautiful that it even stood up to short-range scrutiny.

"You might have been killed," she was murmuring. "You made me strap myself in, and took such a risk yourself."

Every fiber in Fis's being prompted him to stay where he was and let himself be so tenderly fondled. But underneath his headache, the scientist in him continued to function. He scrambled to his feet.

"The chronometer," he gasped.

The remorseless finger was ticking forward.

"Tell me what happened…"

The sharp, urgent note in his voice made Da respond briskly. "The strips went into section with a terrible jerk—worse than those in a really worn out Cabriolet."

"Lubrication," Fis murmured.

"Very likely. It shook all the breath out of me, and sent you flying right across the chamber. You've been unconscious for nearly an hour—"

"An hour!"

Fis grabbed his tools, and started to climb the narrow ladder that led upward through a hatch in the roof of the chamber, toward the radar homing gear in the rocket's nose.

"We should have started using the rocket apparatus," he said, "at least ten minutes ago…"

A shiver ran down Da's spine. She remembered his words about the rocket apparatus, uttered quite calmly in the Museum of Antiquities: "If it doesn't work, we just fly at random through space…" Until when? Until the food ran out and they starved.

She glanced at the anti-gravitational alloy section-handles on the control board. They were snapping one after the other into the neutral position, as Fis, up in the nose of the spaceship, pushed the stiff master-control laboriously over from alloy to rocket, A to R.

A pouring sound came from beneath her feet. The liquid oxygen rushing into its vacuum chamber.

Then the whole spaceship lurched and shuddered. Da clung to a handgrip for support.

Then once more it was still, poised, serene again.

She was just beginning to relax her grip, when a second lurch, worse than the first, made the floor heave.

She had just regained her balance again when she caught sight of Fis's feet, scuttling down the narrow ladder from the overhead hatch.

"I can't get the rocket gear to start," he said. She was surprised to find he was calm, matter-of-fact. He might have been talking about some habit peculiar to Men, the remote Earth species he had studied with such absorbed interest.

"What do you think is the trouble?"

"An impurity in the oxygen, I guess. We scoured the fuel chamber. But in those days their alloys were often imperfect. I dare say there's been some unforeseen electrolytic action, some chemical change."

"You sound very calm about it."

"Would it help to make a fuss?"

"How long have we got?"

"Barring collision with a meteorite, or some sheer bad luck like that—we've got as long as the food in that cupboard lasts."

"And I suppose we are going to pass the time," she said, trying to match his calmness, "learning languages?"

"Or making love," he answered, taking her in his arms.

"At least," she replied, softly, "up here we shan't be interrupted…"

Momentarily they were able to forget their problems, but soon Fis found his brain once again racing over the possibilities.

There were four.

The effect of the anti-gravitational alloy wasn't absolute. There was leakage at the edges, and some permeation of gravitational influence actually through the material. So it was probable that they weren't yet quite out of Mars' gravitational field. Accordingly, the spaceship might slowly be compelled to revolve around Mars, like a sluggish moon.

Or maybe the inertia of the anti-gravitational drive had driven them out of Mars' field and into the edges of the gravitational field of Earth. Here again the pull would probably be too weak to do more than drag them around in an enormous circle, like a minor moon.

Or maybe they would be drawn irresistibly toward the largest and heaviest mass of matter in the solar system—the sun. In which case, sooner or later, they would be sucked into some great incandescent pit of flaming gas on the face of the sun, and be consumed.

Burning up in the sun would be spectacular and poetic compared to the last possible fate—which was to drift in and out of the solar system, a rejected waif, not massive enough to come under the influence of planets or the sun, travelling at random until the two passengers finally starved.

"Let's have a meal," she said. "A wedding breakfast."

"Do we ration out the food?" he asked.

"Let's enjoy our food while we've got it," she said, chopping sweet lichens expertly with a plastic grater.

"Just a moment," he said. "I'll just have another try with the oxygen. You see—it might be sediment, not impurity. And by now—if it is sediment—it might have dropped down to the bottom of the fuel chamber."

She tried to concentrate on chopping lichen for the salad. She tried not to listen or worry or even hope.

The floor lurched. Then went still again. She felt almost sick with disappointment.

It lurched again. More violently, this time. The lurch was followed by a momentary throbbing—a new note, which slowly died away.

Then came a final lurch, which sent her pans and kitchen implements rolling across the floor. The throbbing started anew. This time it trembled dubiously once or twice, but finally was sustained and held its beat.

Fis came down the ladder again, grinning from ear to ear.

She looked up at him, trying hard not to smile, because any smile at such a moment was liable to turn suddenly into tears.

"You might have been more careful," she said, at last, "you've simply ruined our lunch."

The Chairman instructed the most expert telecinegraph operator on Mars to cover the flight of the rocket, using the up-to-date Blue Brain equipment.

People dropped in to watch at intervals during the day. All the gossip and all the speculation in the Martian capital of Centralia was about the young couple flying from Mars to Earth.

The operator was certainly hot stuff. He kept up with the space ship most expertly—only losing it once, when the first attempt to start the oxygen motor caused it to move jerkily out of the screen's range.

It's safe to say that when it was realized that the rocket gear wasn't working, and the news got spread around, half the people in Centralia held their breath. There was talk of sending a resolution of protest to the Global Brains, objecting to the use of an obsolete spaceship, when a delay of a few weeks might have provided an improved one.

Then, after an unendurable wait, the Blue Brain picked up an image that was just a puff of discharged oxygen. By accelerating the finder-speed they were able to catch up with the rocket again. And there, ahead of the rocket, growing larger in the night sky, from the size of a coin to that of an orange, and even greater, until the outlines of continent and ocean could be clearly discerned, was the planet Earth.

The Martians were hourly nearing their destination.

CHAPTER THREE
The Lunatic War

THE war that finally broke out on Earth was totally different from what everyone expected.

Instead of a war between ideologies, it was a war between colors. Yellow and brown man fought white. The whites thought they were going to be able to retain their hold on the black men of Africa, but found instead that Africa was a huge hotbed of color fifth column, hardly worthwhile making an effort to hold. In South Africa, the most developed part, two million whites were quickly swamped by ten million blacks. And elsewhere, the difference in numbers was even more marked and the swamping even quicker.

But basically it was a war between West and East (with a few sideshows like the Brazilian Civil War and the Black insurrection in the southern United States). The ethnic people, yellow and brown, provided the numbers. The white people of Europe and America provided the machines. And, to everyone's surprise, Russia stayed neutral. And that was, of course, inevitable, as she was the only country with a foothold both in Asia and Europe. They sold food and raw materials to both sides, and then folded their hands and waited.

And nor were the horror-weapons much used. Both sides had the atom bomb, so neither dared be the first to employ it. Germ warfare was a double-edged weapon—as effective against the dense, industrialized countries of Europe as against the sprawling lands of Asia. It proved to be a real old-fashioned war, with antiquated weapons like bayonets and poison gas.

And it started in such a silly way.

The border between Burma and Siam, East of the Salween, is rather ill defined. It goes through swampy jungles and barren mountains that are no use to anybody, so the oriental governments concerned, very sensibly leave the actual position of the frontier vague.

But an oilman prospecting under a concession granted by the Siamese Government struck oil near the frontier. Without realizing it, he had actually crossed the frontier, and made his strike in Burma, as he found when he returned to Bangkok to register the claim.

Then the Burmese Government stepped in and nationalized this oil field. The prospector claimed compensation, and his government sent an aircraft carrier from Manila to Bangkok and flew a squadron of jet bombers to Rangoon on a "courtesy mission."

After inspecting the bombers and thinking matters over, the Burmese wondered whether or not they had made a mistake about nationalizing the oil. But before they could change their minds, the Siamese made a claim that the oil-bearing territory was theirs and demanded that Burmese troops withdraw from the frontier. After that, the Burmese Government couldn't climb down, since a favorite way of criticizing an unpopular cabinet minister in Burma is to assassinate him.

So a silly little local war started in the jungles of lower Burma, along the east bank of the Salween River.

When the Americans let the Siamese have arms, the Indians promptly let the Burmese have arms. Soon China was involved and the war spread right across the continent. It started as a frontier war between two oriental peoples, and ended as a world war between races.

At the precise time when the spaceship entered the Earth's atmosphere a gigantic tank-battle was going on across the deserts of Arabia, for the possession of that strategic but arid quadrilateral.

Fis spent much of his time at the small telecinegraph screen the spaceship carried, picking up details of the fighting on Earth. He decided to land the ship on the terraced coffee plantations outside the Yemen port of Mocha—a strategic point in the tank war.

The long, cigar-shaped object came down to Earth in the early hours of the morning. Above was the intensely dark Oriental sky, with the stars burning with unwanted brightness.

Fis opened the hatch and they stepped down, panting lightly as their lungs became adjusted to Earth's atmosphere.

"Look at that red star up there," said Fis. "That's Mars—that's home—"

"It looks an awful long way away," Da answered. She looked around her, sniffed the air. From the south came the perfume of the coffee plantations. From the north, came the clean, sweet, astringent air of the desert.

"I wonder if I shall get to like Earth?" she asked.

"You'd better," he said. "Remember, I promised to destroy the spaceship with the Annihilator—"

He took the oddly shaped pistol from its box, looked at Da.

"But that's our only way back," she said.

"Not quite," he reminded her. "There's that Earth rocket being prepared for flight. Where was it? In Nevada. And those watching us…up there…" he pointed a finger toward Mars, "may send off a relief expedition."

In the Blue Brain, on Mars, the Chairman and the Brain with the roving eye sat side by side, gazing on the telecinegraph screen.

"How much longer is he going to argue," grumbled the Brain, "before he gets rid of that spaceship? We don't want Earthmen getting possession of it, and flying up here to Mars…"

"He'll do it," said the Chairman, "he's a good boy…"

"Besides, he knows we're watching him," said his colleague, a trifle sourly.

In the Arabian night there was a flash and crackle, and the spaceship disintegrated. Nothing was left except odd pieces of plastic that had contained no metal—but the alloy shell had gone for good.

Da commenced to say, "Well, that's that—" but the words were choked from her mouth. The flash of the Annihilator was answered by a sudden glowing artificial star from a Verey pistol, to the north in the desert. And then an artillery barrage started.

The flash of the Annihilator had been taken for a pre-arranged signal by white troops in the desert for their night attack on the Red Sea port of Mocha.

That booming barrage was long-range stuff, lobbed over from a cruiser based on Port Suez, which had sailed down to bombard Mocha from the sea. And it was taken up and echoed by field guns working their way down the terraced plantations. And behind them came the tanks.

From the fortifications of Mocha came a rattle of small-arms, which sounded pitifully small in comparison with the mechanized weapons with which the Arabs and their colored friends were confronted. Then, cantering through the night, came a squadron of cavalry, bearded Oriental horsemen, waving swords and rifles, maddened by smoking hemp, riding straight at the tanks and the certain death which is a Moslem's passport to everlasting paradise.

Ducked down under cover beside a stone wall at the edge of a coffee field, Fis and Da saw the spectacle.

"But they're so brave!" she whispered.

"These Earth people are brave enough," he answered. "But in the wrong causes. Now, don't look any more…"

But peering through her laced fingers, swallowing down the revulsion and horror that welled up in her, Da saw the attack made by horsemen upon tanks.

They rode like madmen toward the lumbering metallic monsters that rolled forward through the night. But the machine guns in the tank turrets chattered, and the cannon revolved and punched away with monotonous precision. And the horsemen were chopped down like weeds slashed by a walking stick.

"Stop it, stop it!" Da breathed.

Fis looked down at the weapon in his hand, and realized he held the key.

He adjusted the range of the Annihilator to maximum. There was a wider flash, the shape of a fishtail. The air, lightening as dawn began to break, was full of a fine dust.

Fis turned to Da with a smile. But she was wrestling with garments from which all the metal buttons, hooks-and-eyes and pins had suddenly disappeared.

"You might have been a little more careful," she said.

"Here's a piece of string," he said, grinning.

"I don't mind you," she said, "It's all those others—" and she pointed north of them, to the place which a few moments before had been a battlefield.

But the men there—those who were still alive—were too busily engaged to bother about Da's predicament.

The tank-men, clothed in a battle-dress and squatting on the meager upholstery of the inside of their tanks, had thundered forward with all the power of mechanized and death-dealing metal. Then in a flash, the tanks had disappeared from under them. They hurtled forward through the choking brown dust, at the velocity of the tank, and came to a headlong stop in the earth below.

But that wasn't the least of it. Their uniform buttons had been made of metal. When they stood up, their trousers fell around their knees. Cannon and machine guns, too, had disintegrated. They had nothing to defend themselves with but their fists.

And the Arabs, thundering toward them, were in little better plight. Scimitars had suddenly melted, leaving nothing but the wooden, or leather, grip. The metal of harness had vanished, pitching many horsemen full tilt. Of rifles, nothing was left except the wooden butt and the little piece of two-by-four inside the butt plate used for cleaning purposes.

The one strategic advantage enjoyed by the Arabs was that their clothing didn't depend on metal buttons.

The opposing sides met fist to fist at the upper edge of the coffee plantation near where Da and Fis sheltered. The fighting was ludicrous and relatively harmless. There might be a few black eyes as a result of it, but there would be few weeping widows.

"I think we've done a good job here," said Da, soft and earnest.

And then from behind them began again the booming of six-inch guns from the bombarding cruiser.

"If I turn the Annihilator in that direction, it will play over the city, too—"

"They'd rather lose a few carving knives," Da suggested, "than be blown to bits…"

Once more the fishtail spark of the Annihilator flashed.

Nobby Clarke had been torpedoed half a dozen times in World War II. He wasn't especially delighted with World War III, so far—but at least the black, brown and yellow men against whom he was fighting had relatively few submarines (though the Japanese were building them fast). He didn't like bombarding a lot of civilians—but at least he, personally, was safe.

Then, one minute he was detonating a six-inch shell, and the next he was swallowing a quart of tepid, salty Red Sea water.

Nobby was never very fond of drinking water at the best of times. He bobbed to the surface, spat out about a mouthful of unswallowed water, and looked around him.

In some ways it had been like being torpedoed. There was the spreading mass of fuel—oil glistening on the surface of the sea—good stuff to swim away from.

And yet being torpedoed was fundamentally different.

Fifty yards away was a life raft, containing practically no metal—already crammed with survivors.

Nobby turned and began a leisurely breaststroke. He was puzzled. It was like being torpedoed—yet again, it wasn't.

First—there was no impact when the torpedo struck.

Second—there was no whirlpool, dragging survivors down into the heart of its maelstrom, as the great bulk of the cruiser sank.

Thirdly—the whistle he kept on a lanyard around his neck, together with a tiny rubber-covered flash lamp (in case he was lost overboard at night) had both disappeared. But the lanyard, and the rubber, were still there.

As he swam, he glanced down at his little finger. A signet ring his wife had given him—with their initials engraved inside. To remind him not to be a bad lad in foreign ports. And the ring, gleaming gold, was still there.

"It must be a new weapon," he thought, as hands reached down from the raft to grab him, "a weapon that attacks steel, and doesn't touch gold."

The ray had not made such an overwhelming difference to the Oriental town of Mocha.

One or two iron balconies had disappeared, dropping potted palms upon the street beneath. A woman, walking down the street with a copper water pot on her shoulder, had been drenched to the skin. The iron doors and grilled windows of the harems were no more, and the eunuch on guard at the door grasped the haft of a spear from which the blade had gone.

A couple of modern ships in the harbor had simply disintegrated. Sailing vessels held together with nails suddenly became a mass of floating planks.

But a few ancient dhows still floated. For they were made in the original way—pegged with wooden pegs and the planks sewn with coir rope, because the ancient Arab traders believed that using metal in the construction of a ship invited the Evil Eye.

It was on one of these dhows—one of the few vessels in the world capable of standing up against the Annihilator, that Da and Fis sailed north up the Red Sea.

They passed struggling men in the water, left behind them a battlefield, where men fought not with weapons but with tooth and claw, a city where the only implements for carrying on agriculture were a few stone hoes and wooden spades.

"North of here, near the so-called Suez Canal, is an airfield," said Fis. "The rate at which I can bring battles to an end will be speeded up, once I can get into the air. He was delighted with his success outside Mocha—he had feelings similar to those of a mother who with difficulty has managed to take away from her child a dangerous toy.

Intelligence Officers from the Whites' G.H.Q. at Medina reached the scene of battle toward afternoon.

There had been a few casualties in the hand-to-hand encounter—stones had started to be used. But by and large both sides had enjoyed the scrap, and were ending up firm friends.

"Fraternizing!" gasped the major from Intelligence, as he saw Arab and White, like two sides after a rugby match, sit down and drink water from goatskins, the metal water bottles of the troops having gone along with their buttons and the nails holding their boots together.

The major walked on to the battlefield, hand on his Webley. "This is war, not a pantomime!" he said sharply. "Fall in—full marching order."

One man, the habit of obedience too strong for him, stood erect, and promptly his trousers fell down.

Another stepped forward, and the boots fell from his feet— he cursed as the hot rock touched his bare flesh.

"You were sent here for a battle, not a picnic," fumed the major. "Now tell me—are these men your prisoners? If not, you're guilty of fraternizing—"

A surviving captain, his insignia disintegrated, attempted a salute, one hand holding up his trousers, while the other went to the brim of his hat.

"The fact is, sir," he explained, "we've nothing to fight with. The other side is using some diabolical weapon—"

An old, dignified Arab came forward, touching brow, lips and breast in greeting.

"The colored people of the world," he said, "use no diabolical weapon. We thought this mysterious weapon must be yours, not ours."

"Weapon?" barked the major.

"If I say it seems to be a ray that dissolves metal, I suppose you won't believe me," said the captain, "but it's a plain fact."

News of this revolutionary weapon, which had made a brief appearance in the field at Mocha, caused a high-level flap on both sides.

Diplomatic overtures in Moscow, both official and unofficial, drew a blank. If the Russians had the weapon, they weren't going to admit it. If they didn't have it, they weren't going to deny it. They were as much in the dark as everybody else.

Meanwhile, both banks of the Red Sea were afflicted. In the squalid little coastal ports that hug the unlovely coastlines of that part of the world, metal disintegrated and disappeared. The menace of the ray spread slowly northwards at the pace of an epidemic.

They had bacteriologists, metallurgists—every sort of specialist except mind readers—rushing down to Mocha. They analyzed the dust, but got no useful information.

One fact that emerged—gold had not been affected by the ray. For his revealing of this information to Naval Intelligence, Able Seaman Nobby Clarke, survivor from the sunken cruiser, was promoted to the rate of Leading Seaman, only to be broken down a fortnight later for being drunk and disorderly on rice alcohol in Aden.

Finally, the confronting generals in Arabia arranged a private and unofficial truce. Then each side—waking up to the obvious facts at last—started sending reconnaissance airplanes over the Red Sea, scanning every inch, looking for the submarine (Japanese, American, Russian—nobody knew) that was carrying the ray.

Da and Fis were having a lovely time aboard the dhow. At first the "water" (a mixture of oxygen and hydrogen, with various impurities) with which the "sea" on Earth was filled, rather baffled Fis. It had a much lower specific gravity than the canal-liquid on Mars. But the principles of navigation are much the same, all the universe over. And life with Da on a dhow was much less nerve-wracking than the voyage in the spaceship had been. They had time to relax and tell each other in detail the history of their respective lives. Also Fis, with an eye to eventualities, used the opportunity to instruct Da in basic Earth languages. She could learn with surprising rapidity, and was soon making pretty speeches in English with a fascinating Martian accent.

But they conscientiously swept the ray in both port and starboard directions at intervals, each day, devastating both coastlines, and also sinking any metallic vessels that might be sent in pursuit of them.

The one real snag was that their progress could be pinpointed by the manner in which the devastated area kept creeping slowly toward Port Suez.

The first reconnaissance aircraft were a serious problem.

The odds were they would take no particular notice of a native dhow—unless something their attention was drawn to it. And downing an aircraft with the ray would be precisely the thing that would do most to attract attention, because the reconnaissance aircraft kept in close touch with the shore.

In actual fact, the first time Fis used the ray on a plane was a mistake. He couldn't even clear himself of the suspicion that a trace of jealousy had played its part in his use of the ray.

Up until that particular day, the various scout planes had always kept at a great altitude. But on this day one started a new technique that Fis and Da hadn't previously seen—wave-hopping. The pilot had picked up the dhow on radar, and flew low to investigate.

And it so happened that Da had chosen that particular time for sunbathing. For one thing, Fis, as a student of Earth conditions, had realized that they would benefit by having skins less pink-white. A faint tinge of brown sunburn—so that they could pass either as swarthy whites or light coloreds—would be of great value. For another thing, Da liked sunbathing anyway, and had only the scantiest of clothing on so as to get as near an all-over tan as decency permitted.

Of course, the pilot's eyes, after a first glimpse, popped out of his head. Just to make sure he wasn't dreaming or having visions, he banked his plane and came in for a second look, a good one this time, at nearly zero altitude and nearly at stalling speed.

Fis, who had just come on deck, saw the pilot's craning neck and gaping eyes, and saw the cause of it, as Da tried to duck for cover under the dhow's triangular sail. And he happened to have the Annihilator in his hand.

The next thing the pilot knew, the plane he was flying in had totally disintegrated, while he himself continued at a velocity of eighty miles an hour, describing an arc until he hit the sea with a horrible smack.

"Fis—" said Da, a look of horror on her face, "that was just what we agreed not to do!"

"I must confess," he said grimly, "I went 'bad' for a moment, when I saw him looking at you like that."

"Oh, look," Da cried, "he's alive!" It seemed miraculous, but the man in the water was stirring, and his life jacket had inflated.

A look of relief washed over Da's face. She looked sternly back at Fis. "Since we're on Earth," she said, "we'll have to relax the rules, I suppose. Because if I send you to Coventry for going bad, I shall be sending myself to Coventry at the same time.

"I hope he can swim," said Fis, hauling on the main sheet, and letting the wind from the south fill the big lateen sail.

It would be a pity if the flyer drowned, but an even bigger pity if Fis and Da got captured. Fis remembered some of the things he had seen on H.T., in Mars, of what happened to captives in World War II. He shuddered at the thought of what either side—white, black, yellow, or brown—would do to Da if she fell into their hands.

A radar check had been kept on the aircraft that disintegrated, and soon an air-sea-rescue patrol flew down from Tor, on the Gulf of Suez. After several hours' search, they found the airman, floating partly conscious on the sea. By then the triangular sail of the dhow was a mere dot to the northward.

Ashore at Tor they fed him brandy until he revived well enough to tell his story, with a couple of doctors in attendance.

"I was wave-hopping, in accordance with latest orders, and keeping my eyes peeled for the giant enemy submarine that people are talking about. And suddenly I came across a dhow—"

"Well. What's surprising about that?"

"On the fo'c'sle of the dhow—you know, the raised part where the natives say their prayers at noon—was a woman with long hair. The most beautiful woman I have ever seen."

"Arab?"

"I don't know, sir."

"How was she dressed, then?"

"That's just the point, sir. She hadn't enough clothing on to tell. And I mean to say, naturally, I banked and came back for a second look. And when she saw me, she vanished. Then next thing I knew, the aircraft had vanished also in a puff of smoke, and I was heading for the drink at high speed."

"A beautiful woman, eh?" The doctors exchanged dubious glances.

"Yes, sir. I know it sounds incredible, sir."

"Did you notice the—*ahem*—the lower part of her body?"

"Not specially, sir. Not more than one would on such a short acquaintance."

"You didn't happen to notice whether she had legs or a cod's tail?" one of the doctors said with a slight smile.

"No, sir. Definitely human. It was a woman, not a mermaid."

The two doctors turned and walked out.

"Heatstroke," said one, categorically.

"Possibly battle neurosis," said the other, with equal emphasis.

They went out into the passage and tossed a coin up to decide which diagnosis it was to be.

But Intelligence, just to make doubly sure, put a man into Port Suez to look out for a dhow carrying a beautiful woman. So it was just as well that Da went ashore in the clothes of an Arab male with her hair tied up in a turban. Fis also had on a semi-Oriental costume.

Port Suez was a frontier town. To the south was Africa—now totally in the hands of the blacks. To the East, a great battle was raging to decide which army held the waterless semi-continent of Arabia. If the battle were lost, the forces of the colored races would flood through the Middle East to the Mediterranean seaboard, and then it would not be long before Europe was overwhelmed.

As they walked toward the airport, Fis thought of his plans, and let Da Overthink them. This was much safer than actually talking about them and perhaps being overheard speaking in a strange lingo.

His duty was to do as much damage with the Annihilating Ray in a minimum of time. He could coast about the battlefronts and have a local or temporary effect on one battle or the other. But the place where a blow would really have the greatest effect would be in the industrialized part of each side's war camps. Most of which were located in the big cities of Western Europe, North America, Japan, and China. It would be a real knockout blow at the industrial heart of each side, and if it did not stop the war, it would at least change its character. In a short space of time, they would be reduced to fighting with bows and arrows—if they still fought at all.

But to deliver such a blow meant travelling halfway around the globe—and that meant acquiring an aircraft.

Fis had at one time made a special study of the primitive modes of aerial transport that existed on Earth. He was quite confident that, given an aircraft, he could fly it. And the easiest way might be to simply walk onto an airfield and steal the most readily available one.

The Port Suez airfield was occupied at that time by the U.S. Air Force.

Da, while walking ashore, complained that her turban was too hot on her scalp. They had made it safely through the harbor; and there was no longer any special point in her masquerading as a man, so Fis told her she could take it off if she wanted to.

She stopped at the roadside and wasted several valuable minutes untwisting the turban, braiding her hair and arranging it in a suitable womanly style. Then she wound the turban-cloth around the waist of her garment, as a cummerbund, so arranged that the skirts of her garment were lifted to reveal several inches of trim ankle.

Fis had to admit that the effect was worth looking around at. But just then they weren't particularly anxious to draw attention to themselves.

Da Overthought that Fis wasn't specially pleased with her appearance and she put it down to mild possessiveness. So when they passed a group of American airmen, and they whistled, she turned and bestowed on them a long drawn-out, glittering smile.

That smile brought them more than they bargained for. Amidst appreciative cries and sundry objurgations of a more or less flattering character, the Americans ran to their jeep. The engine coughed into life and seconds later they rumbled toward Fis and Da.

This was when Fis made a huge error in judgement.

He had never studied life on the American continent in great detail—in the Blue Brain that had been Daren's special sector. He didn't realize that the Americans' enthusiastic shouts, as they drove full-tilt toward Da, were merely a bawdy tribute to the beauty of her womanhood.

And Fis—to whom the very idea of weapons had been, until a short while ago, totally repugnant—had only one effective means of defending himself.

He shouted to Da, "Run!" He then drew the Annihilator from inside his caftan. The blue spark—at short range—flashed and spluttered. The jeep was reduced into upholstery, four rubber tires and a big splash of petrol, and the Americans, minus buttons and side arms, went sprawling in the dust.

"Get him!" shouted an officer.

Clutching their pants, the bruised Americans pounded after Fis. Da had several yards head start, but she had the bad luck to pick a cross-country route that was intersected by watercourses.

Fis himself got clean away and hid crouching in a ditch.

From far to the right of him he could hear a sound that chilled his blood—the faint shrilling screams of Da, cornered among the watercourses. Followed by the triumphant roar of the American airmen as they captured her and took her off in triumph to the camp near the airfield.

Half an hour later, with a roar, a great six-engined jet bomber took off from the field.

It circled over the flat, watercourse-intersected fields where Fis, carrying with him the Annihilator, had gone to earth.

As the bomber got overhead at this point, all but two of the engines were cut. The bomber cruised around near stalling speed with a minimum of noise.

Then, with the loudness of some god speaking out of the sky, came words in some language unknown either to the fellahin working in the fields, or to the soldiers at the airfield who heard them. They were spoken in a rich contralto, and amplified many times by powerful radio apparatus.

The voice was that of Da, and the language was Martian.

She said, "They've got me up here in this flying machine. It works by engines, as ours on Mars used to in prehistoric times. I'm tied up, and they have threatened to treat me badly. They have told me to tell you to yield up to them the Annihilator. Now I say to you—"

Just then there came a scream, terminating in a grunt, as if someone had struck her.

For a moment Fis was baffled. Then he remembered the way Da had screamed when the airmen had captured her—indeed, he was never likely to forget that sound. And this particular amplified scream was quite different. They were trying to bring pressure to bear on him by suggesting that Da was being subjected to brutality. The voice that screamed was not Da's voice, but somebody else's, added on after her words were finished. Was Da in the plane at all?

They would rely on his belief that she was there, in order to protect themselves. Otherwise no airman would care to fly in a metal plane in pursuit of a fugitive who had the power to make metal disappear.

He looked down at the Annihilator in his hand, and up at the slowly circling bomber. Regretfully he decided that the risk was greater than he dared to take.

Suddenly a man's voice, greatly magnified by radio, echoed across the terrain.

"This woman tells us that you speak better English than she does. At this moment she is certainly regretting waging war on our forces. And that will go for you, too, if you don't surrender. We'll chase you across Egypt if we have to, but we *will* get you sooner or later—and it *won't* be nice. Now why not be a reasonable guy and give yourself up? That's a honey of a dame you're travelling with. I'll see she isn't ill-treated anymore—I'll give you my personal assurance. Just give yourself up to any White picket or military post…"

But Fis had long since ceased to listen to the voice that boomed over his head. He was scampering across country in the direction of the airfield, keeping under cover as much as possible.

He was cautiously optimistic that they hadn't really ill-treated Da. For one thing, Americans had the reputation for being one of the more civilized races on Earth, with a high respect for womanhood. For another thing, they had no need actually to ill-treat her, providing they could frighten him by making believe they had done so.

In any event, either she was in the giant bomber, or still on the airfield. Either way, she had to be rescued.

And so, while the magnified, dehumanized voice overhead threatened and cajoled, Fis pushed his way across the irrigated fields toward the concrete runway with its barbed wire fence.

CHAPTER FOUR
The Flying Annihilator

A BARBED wire entanglement was to Fis a very minor obstacle. He reduced the range of the Annihilator to near its minimum, and just wiped out enough of the barbed wire to walk through comfortably—his sandals scrunching on the brown dust.

So this was an airfield.

The white and black control tower, the broad runways, at right angles to each other. The unceasing roar of engines. A very crude way of flying, really. Aeronautics on Earth had taken the wrong turn when airships were discarded. Ever since then, an enormous amount of valuable petroleum, a substance diminishing measurably each year on Earth, had been used up merely to get these flying machines off the ground. Whereas if they had been more patient, and not given up the search for a substance to counteract gravity (after the dangerous failure of gases like hydrogen and helium) they might have struck on Martian anti-gravitational alloy, which uses gravity itself as a motive power. No engines, no fuel wasted, no noise, smell, fuss, or danger.

Eventually, Fis reflected, aeronautical technique on Earth would get out of its blind alley. But meantime, an airfield was a place of noisy pandemonium, besides the ever-present danger through fire and crashes.

He ducked down between two buildings of mud-brick native houses, which had been included in the perimeter when the airfield was built and never demolished.

The big bomber was coming in to land.

Was Da on board, or was she not?

He watched the bomber come down, its huge double wheels emerging from the wings. It touched down on the runway and finally—after a long run—came to a halt.

A hatch in the side opened, and down stepped a man in uniform, with a peaked cap. Down to him was handed a microphone trailing on a lead, and some radio apparatus. He started to walk across to a building made of whitewashed concrete.

Observing where the man went, Fis meanwhile continued to watch the plane. After a pause, the pilot got out, unbuckling his helmet and pushing goggles onto his forehead. And after that— no one. The mechanics started to manhandle the plane toward its hangar, aided by a small electric tractor. Evidently they had made a record of Da's voice to lure him, but left Da herself on the ground.

The pilot walked toward the concrete building.

It was near sunset. Fis waited amid the mud huts until the sun went down. Twilight is very brief in Egypt. Soon the night was at its darkest in the hour before the Orient moon rose.

The concrete building was about seventy yards away. Even for Martians as intelligent (and as much in sympathy) as Da and Fis, seventy yards is extreme range for Overthinking.

But, under cover of darkness, Fis walked to the rear of the concrete building, and tried to Overthink Da.

She was sleeping. The even ripple of a brain contentedly asleep confirmed that she was both in this building and unharmed. No one who had been maltreated would sleep so soundly.

As Fis concentrated on thoughts of her, he sensed how her sleep was being first disturbed, then brought to an end.

Then her brain, too, began to concentrate. Soon messages of reassurance and hope, and plans for escape, were flashing from brain to brain with swiftness and secrecy.

The guard looked through the window of the cells to the girl inside.

Some looker.

They said she was a Colored, though. And there was no doubt she was an enemy—the Intelligence branch had been grilling her all the time from when she had been captured to when she fell asleep.

Her English was mediocre—but the scornful glances from those handsome flashing eyes spoke more than words. They had forced her to make a dicta-phone record and then cut it off when the glint in her eyes made them think she was double-crossing them. The message had then been boomed across at the runaway, in her lingo, whatever it was. But the result—nil.

Now she was waking up. Tossing back her magnificent head of hair, pushing back the blankets, sitting upright, her face serious, as if she were praying or remembering past misdeeds.

Some looker.

They could do with a dame like that to make propaganda films for the war effort in Hollywood. Except that she was a Colored, and, of course, all the Coloreds had been purged from Hollywood as potential traitors.

She was awake. She was getting out of bed, putting on her sandals.

"You getting up already?" said the guard, slightly more friendly. "It ain't morning yet."

Her answer, too, wasn't as hostile as her earlier talk had been. "My people don't sleep much."

"Your people? Where do you come from, then, ma'am?"

She smiled—the sort of smile that sends a young man rocking back on his heels. "My home is a red star way up in the sky," she said.

A red star, huh, thought the guard. *I'll have to remember to tell the Intelligence officer that. She's practically admitted she's a red.*

"I should appreciate," she said, "a drink of water."

"Sure," said the guard, "sure thing. There's iced water across in the orderly room. This is an American camp, ma'am, and there's the latest of everything. Iced water, magazines, air conditioning—" And talking rather like a salesman (which was what he had been in civilian life) he walked across toward the guardroom door.

The holding cells where Da was confined had been barred from ceiling to floor, the iron bars being set in concrete.

From outside in the night came a very faint crackle, like an electric spark. And the cell bars were suddenly not there any longer.

What was more, the ferro-concrete bars in the fabric wall and floor had also disappeared. Frightening-looking cracks began to appear in the structure of the building.

Da ran for the door, just as the young guard appeared with a cup in his hand.

"What's this!" he exclaimed, reaching out a hand to grab at her.

Not hesitating, Da dived for the front door through which she had been brought.

His hand, grabbing at random, closed on her blouse. The following jerk tore away a couple of square feet of the flimsy material. There was a brief glimpse of rounded, coffee colored flesh...

Then she had disappeared into the night.

"No shame, these Coloreds," he muttered to himself, reflecting that any American girl would have squealed in embarrassment in such circumstances. And without thinking, he mopped his sweating brow with the cloth souvenir still clutched in his hand.

As the alarm was raised, the men in the guardroom went to the weapons rack to grab rifles from the clips. But the rifles were just odd bits and pieces and a heap of dust.

"Don't touch that dust," cried one of the soldiers excitedly, "it might be poisonous."

In fact, it was perfectly harmless, but the guards couldn't have known. They tumbled out onto the airfield perimeter as cracks went through the walls and the whole building started to sway. They shrank away, and as Da and Fis pounded together through the night, the men who should have been chasing after them were tiptoeing around the rapidly disintegrating guardroom, like children playing a complicated game of hopscotch, trying to avoid the brown dust that lay everywhere.

The aircraft was a three-seater torpedo-bomber reconnaissance aircraft of the Navy Air Force. Fis had picked it out for two reasons—it had the longest cruising range of any aircraft on the field, and it had a bomb-hatch.

He made a nerve-wracking, yet creditable take-off for a man whose knowledge of Earth aeronautics was based on a theoretical reconstruction made with the help of a telecinegraph. But since he had broken every air-traffic-control regulation on the airfield, he was spotted right away. There was soon a fighter roaring after them, and the fighter opened fire with its multiple cannon.

Fis didn't want to harm any of these Earth creatures if he could help it. If only they'd been reasonable! But here they were, firing explosive shells at him.

He switched on the automatic pilot, then crawled down to the bomb bay and slid it back. The chill night air gushed into the aircraft. Da, whose clothing had never recovered from her tussle with the guard, said, "I'll be getting...what's the beastly disease they contract on Earth? Pneumonia?"

Fis adjusted the ranging apparatus on the Annihilator. He leaned out of the bomb bay into a burst of rushing air so that the disintegrative ray of the Annihilator would miss his own aircraft.

A flash and crackle, and the pursuing fighter aircraft vanished in a puff of dust.

The pilot hurtled down like a stone. And beside him fell a smaller bundle—his parachute. It had been held on by a metal buckle, which had disappeared at the same time as the structure of the aircraft.

"Poor young man," Da murmured in sadness. She was getting fond of the Earth creatures—even though some of their ways were beastly. Taken as individuals they were all right— collectively they were often horrible.

"There's another plane starting to take off," she added, looking back.

So Fis turned the aircraft, banking steeply around. Then he scrambled down into the bomb bay once more. This time he increased the range of the ray.

He saved a few lives this time. Those pursuit planes were now just patches of dust on the ground, impotent to pursue the flying Martian.

In fact, the only danger came from a full petrol bowser, which, like everything else containing metal, came under the influence of the ray. Such a quantity—gallons and gallons of petrol—made for an immediate fire danger.

"Now," said Fis, "we head for the industrial heart of the Whites' area. By the time we finish, there won't be an industrial plant capable of production."

The aircraft crossed the Mediterranean, potting ships one after the other. Very soon, as word of the secret weapon spread, not a vessel would leave port. At least if they sank in harbor they could swim ashore.

Soon Fis and Da swept up the Italian peninsula. The factories of Milan and Turin, the shipyards of Genoa, all succumbed. They made a detour to the industrial areas of Lyons and Barcelona. Then they headed for the Ruhr.

They landed near Strasbourg and were able to convince a ground personnel member at the air-station into refueling their plane. Da's feminine charms had certainly helped. They were soon back in the air.

It was over the Ruhr that a great idea occurred to Fis.

"I've been studying this little gadget of your father's," he said. "Upon my word, he was a genius. Simple, portable, and like all great ideas, capable of development. But of course on Mars he couldn't have had such a chance as Earth affords us to give it a thorough testing."

"What are you getting at?"

"The range of this ray. There's no reduction of its power—even at maximum range. No effective reduction, that is. Now I suggest that we modify the Annihilator by increasing the upward limit of the ray. A ray with a twenty-five thousand-mile range will go right around the Earth—"

"And is that good? Do you think that's really what we should do?"

"If it works it will be a godsend. One flick of the trigger and our work on Earth is done."

"Then home again," she said. "I know of a flat that's vacant, within easy reach of the Blue Brain. You could be near your work—" And then she realized there was only a slim chance of their getting back to Mars and stopped in mid-sentence with her mouth open.

The Whites had been tracing the course of the Martians' bomber by the belt of devastation that it left on each side of its course.

There were hurried conferences, and all sorts of bright ideas put forward for dealing with the menace. But what use were interceptor aircraft, ack-ack guns, any of the devices of modern war against a weapon that merely dissolved the metal of which they were principally made?

They tried death-or-glory boys using oxygen apparatus, and flying high above Fis and Da, hoping to swoop down. But that was a complete failure.

They got the Intelligence report through the usual channels from GHQ Arabia Deserta, about the imperviousness of gold to the ray. One bright young staff officer urged them to cast some ack-ack guns of gold bullion. But even after he had talked over the scoffers, the Treasury stepped in and informed him that gold reserves were far too important a munition of war to be wasted in that particular way.

A proposed mesh of gold net in the path of the aircraft was held to be wasteful and absurd. Then new reports started to come through that worried Military Intelligence even more…

The range of the anti-metallic destruction was widening.

It started in the Ruhr. The whole area around Dortmund and Essen went in one devastating blow. Then the probing, destructive fingers of the ray started to reach out even farther. The Saar, Lille, even as far as Chemnitz and Silesia, came under the influence.

And then the first reports began to come from Britain that the metal rot had set in there, too. It hit Dover first. One moment the cranes on the piers were there, the next moment they had disappeared. Ships in the harbor and docks were floating peaceably at anchor one minute, the next they were a mass of floating timber and struggling survivors.

The overhead cableway that brings coal down from the Kentish coalfield to the harbor arm disappeared in a puff of dust.

To keep a right of way open, every noon a train preceded by a man with a red flag puffs along a railway track on the promenade. Generally they are followed by a troop of fascinated small boys. But when the ray hit that locomotive it dropped driver and fireman neatly on the track. They had to roll quickly out of the way to avoid the piles of glowing coals now burning ahead of them, which had dropped straight out of the firebox on to the tar macadam.

A squad of Seaforth Highlanders were drilling on the barrack square in Dover Castle. One moment there was a disciplined body of men, the next moment a panic-stricken crowd in fancy dress, trying to stop their kilts from dropping off.

Churches and ancient buildings with lead roofs suffered particularly. One minute there was a sound roof, the next there was a hole, brought about much quicker than even the most expert of lead-thieves could accomplish.

The Mayor of Dover got quickly on the telephone to Whitehall. But of course copper was no more impervious to the ray than steel. The phone lines were ruined. So were the telegraph wires. So were trains, buses, cars and cycles. Finally the Mayor had to commandeer a horse from a hackney stables, and send a messenger to ride up the historic Dover road with a dispatch to 10 Downing Street.

And the dispatch itself was written with a quill pen.

The rider cantered off about an hour before Fis and Da, their fingers crossed, started to carry out the final modification, which would give the ray a range of at least one hemisphere, and perhaps the best part of the other.

"Wouldn't it be nice," said Da, "if it got rid of everything except that Earth spaceship which is standing in Nevada, waiting to take us home again."

"You can forget about Nevada," Fis answered. "How are you going to cross the Atlantic Ocean, once all the metal ships are sunk?"

Da's mouth dropped once more. "I never thought of that," she said, and looked skywards, as much as to say, "I hope they are following the pair of us on telecinegraph."

And they were.

The exploits of Fis and Da had become, not only the most fascinating scientific experiment ever carried out by Martians, but also something in which everyone felt involved.

The mass of the Martian population hadn't been so excited about anything since that series of experiments a couple of centuries ago, which had succeeded in putting twenty years on the length of the average life by means of injections into the connective tissue.

The Chairman explained it thus: "On Earth you have a society that is based on the use of metal. But now metal is being withdrawn from it. What will the outcome be? There are two things to consider. On the one hand, mankind has gotten so used to enjoying the benefits of his planet—metals, food, fuel, reasonable climatic conditions—that he takes them for granted. He even wastes his time in barbarities like war, instead of getting on with the task of developing his resources for more beneficial purposes. On the other hand, he's quite an intelligent being— for a sub-Martian. Imitative, with a crude and limited capacity for cooperating with his fellows. He may rise to the challenge. And I rather think he will.

"And our two Martian citizens, who are risking their lives to carry the experiment through? Any citizen of Mars is of priceless value. I don't need to say how we value even the humblest person who contributes to the common good, not to speak of people as gifted and courageous as Fis and Da. I may as well tell you that we are already building a squadron of rockets of an improved pattern to bring them back home—"

"And a good thing too," said one of the Global Brains, who was of a slightly cynical frame of mind; "I will tell you bluntly, if we let anything happen to that pair, not a soul on Mars will vote us back into office next year—"

And another Brain, weary from spending eight days without sleep disentangling a traffic jam on the Canals, murmured, "You almost make that prospect sound tempting," and promptly fell asleep in his council chair.

The British Government made a serious error about the Annihilating Ray. Not trusting the good sense of the people, it kept the news dark.

As an island, Britain was easy to seal off from the continent. So, in time of war, the Government found it easy to keep the people from the true knowledge of the facts.

Now Britain would pay dearly for it.

Various scraps of gossip about a secret weapon had drifted into the country through odd channels. Some said it was the Coloreds, others the Russians.

In some extraordinary way this secret weapon interfered with metal production, or metal supply. That much was generally known. There was a great deal of speculation, but no one was very worried. For one thing, in this war Britain had been a long way from the front line. The British hadn't really begun to take the war seriously yet. Having no color problem at home, they ran no risk of something like the Americans' southern states' insurrection. In fact, as usual, many Britons felt a sneaking sympathy for their enemy.

News about the destruction at Dover was just spreading through London in a fantastic wave of speculation when the ray, now at its new maximum range, struck the British capital.

Just imagine trying to prepare a meal in a kitchen from which all the metal has disappeared!

Quite apart from the leak of coal gas from vanished pipes, the pots and pans themselves would be no more. It wouldn't be possible to peel a potato or boil a kettle. An oven would be a thing of the past. Poking the fire would be impossible.

Multiply that situation several million fold, and this was now what the city of London was now like.

The cast-iron bridges dropped spectacularly into the Thames, and the ferro-concrete ones quickly followed them, under the weight of foot passengers. Double-decker buses became tangled mounds of men and women, half clothed, suddenly dropped violently on top of each other. The whole network of underground tunnels and railway track beneath London became a sudden hell. People travelling between one station and another had to tramp for miles in order to find daylight, often only to be drowned by sewage or gassed by leaking mains. In the East and West Ends, hysteria began to spread.

Unfortunately for Fis and Da, they began to come to the bleak realization that, though their efforts would undoubtedly save millions of lives by reducing the global war effort to a fraction of what it was, and that by removing mankind's advanced weapons of war they would also remove any future threat to Mars itself, they were still undoubtedly causing many lives to be lost with their world-wide destruction of Earth's metals. Planes in flight, autos or trains at high speed, people on high floors of large buildings—it was simply unavoidable.

There was a profound grimness between them as they went about their work. Great Britain was hit particularly hard.

In London, the Cabinet appointed a temporary military overseer. The Cabinet, in fact, it couldn't understand what had happened. At the Cabinet Room in Downing Street, one half of the Cabinet (a coalition) was accusing the other half, the Minister of War was on his knees in prayer, and the Under Secretary of State for Public Abuses was getting quietly drunk out of the Prime Minister's whisky decanter.

The military overseer, a veteran general from Liverpool, quickly grasped the elements of the situation. He rushed reliable troops, armed with nightsticks, to Covent Garden and Billingsgate, and to the food warehouses in the docks, so as to control the food supply—on which everything else would hinge. The troops went on their mission with a will as soon as they had managed to tie up their trousers with string, and loot enough hand-sewn pairs of shoes from the West End shops to make marching possible.

However, owing to the breakdown in communications, Scotland Yard couldn't be informed of the military overseer's action. When the police (their trousers, too, tied up with string) heard the news of a mob dressed in something approximating to military uniform, raiding the markets with sticks in their hands, the Assistant Commissioner mobilized all available men, and rushed them on foot from the Embankment to Covent Garden and Billingsgate, where they arrived quite footsore, their boots having come to bits en route.

So the first effect of the ray was a pitched battle from the best of intentions between the guardians of public order—those in khaki fighting those in blue. Meanwhile, thousands of citizens looked on and drew their own confused conclusions.

The meat, fish and vegetable porters, seeing the police fight the soldiers at a time when the survival of London depended on the rationing of food, called an immediate trade union meeting. They elected a committee to control food supply and appointed pickets to see that food stocks were not interfered with.

A building in the West End, built mainly of stone, accommodated a meeting that was held of the best brains in England. Generals, high-ranking civil servants, diplomats, and important men in the City heatedly argued how the country was to be saved. Monocles gleamed and moustaches bristled.

"The position," commented a representative from the Foreign Office, who having captained the Wall Game at Eton some years before was treated with exceptional respect, "is simple. There isn't an ounce of metal left in London. When every match at present in London has been struck, no one will be able to light a fire without the aid of the Boy Scouts. When all the fuel in London is burned, we shall all shiver. When all the food is gone, we shall all starve—"

At that moment a messenger arrived with the news that the workers at the main markets had elected committees, seized the food, and appointed pickets, even though both police and military had been sent to stop something like that from happening.

"You see what is happening?" said a high-ranking Bishop. "Stark, raving Bolshevism…"

"'This is serious, terribly serious," one of the Generals added. "The common citizens are getting out of hand."

In the pause that followed, the calm, level voice of one of London's leading citizens and war heroes could be heard—a man named Fortescue, whose exploits in the early months of World War III had gained him much fame. He had been responsible for getting the white population out of Johannesburg and marching them down to the frontier of Portuguese East Africa. He had followed that by a mission to the Emperor of Abyssinia, to remind him of the help given by the Whites in recovering his throne. That mission had failed, though, because the people in Abyssinia seemed too backward and primitive to distinguish clearly between Italians and other sorts of Whites, such as Englishmen.

"The first speaker made a fundamental mistake," Fortescue asserted. "Not only is there metal in London, there is, in fact, a number of tons of metal. It is probably the last reserve of metal in England—and that metal is gold. I came straight here from the Bank—after having placed the Yeomen of the Guard around the vault. They are armed with bows and arrows from the armory in the Tower—perhaps the last effective weapons left in London, apart from the knobkerries and boomerangs in the Museum of Ethnology."

"Stout fella," murmured an approving voice.

"Now that great store of gold—the only considerable store in England—will enable its possessors to dominate the country. We have to think of the country's good, gentlemen. We are those specially fitted to rule—and unless we act swiftly—well, you have heard what the mob has already done in Billingsgate—"

There was a staccato grunting of "Hear, hear," around the room.

And the Gentlemen of England sallied forth, armed with sticks and stones, moustaches bristling, monocles gleaming, upper lips stiff, and headed east toward the Bank of England and the Mint.

Along Whitehall they were joined by a group of high-ranking civil servants, and one or two chairborne Army officers from the War Office. As they passed through Trafalgar Square, a few admirals marched through Admiralty Arch and joined them. Somerset House and Bush House added their quotas of civil servants. Lawyers came from the Inns of Court. Fleet Street was disappointing—the journalists obviously intended to sit on the fence and see which side won. And from the City came many a pinstripe-suited hero to fight for the things that made old England what she was.

They were numerous enough and disciplined enough to push their way through the near-hysterical and now hungry crowds, and head for Threadneedle Street.

The City was in chaos. Ferro-concrete buildings more than three stories high were a sheer deathtrap. Of course, New York would be much worse, as Londoners kept reminding themselves.

The average Londoners simply couldn't understand what was happening at first. Then, having comprehended the scope of the disaster, they began to adjust themselves and wait for word from the authorities. There would certainly be some word from the Government in the noon editions. But the noon editions didn't appear, because the presses were sheer heaps of dust. And though the pubs that drew their beer direct from wooden casks were able to function—at least while supplies lasted—there was not a meal to be bought anywhere. Bald-headed and dignified men fought with umbrella sticks, spilling blood over the right to a packet of sandwiches.

As Fortescue led his men past the Stock Exchange, and deployed them skillfully for an attack on the Bank, from within the sacred portals a cry went up, "'Ere they come!" and the body of high-ranking officials were greeted with a shower of brickbats, so well aimed that it instantly created three vacancies in the House of Lords.

"The Reds!" gasped a Bishop.

But it wasn't the Reds. It was the street vendors, the unemployed, even petty criminals and con men. Yes—collectively they were known as "the Spivs" and they were comprised of all those best equipped to deal with such a crisis on a raw survival level. They had food-stocks mainly of fruit or vegetables. They had an organization. They were used to acting in their own defense, without too much consideration for law and order. And so while the honest citizens at first were baffled and puzzled, the Spivs' reaction, right away, was: "What's in this for us?"

Of course, there were certain short-term gains by some of the looters. There were the metal-frame shop windows that suddenly collapsed, saving people with smash-and-grab instincts the trouble of pushing a brick through them. And it was this smash-and-grab technique that helped the Spivs make the initial discovery...

Gold was untouched.

And so when the great realization dawned on Spivs here and there, scattered throughout the East and West Ends, every Spiv in London converged upon the Bank of England.

Choice of a leader was decided between two brawny local Spivs named Bert and Gus. Both were two very adept heavyweight boxers. In a short but savage fight, Gus kayoed Bert with a lightning uppercut. Bert's left leg quivered as he lay unconscious. Gus took immediate command. Not much later the "gentlemen of England" appeared on the scene, marching in battle array from the West End.

Prior to that there had been a short skirmish between the Spivs and the Yeomen of the Guard. The battle only lasted about five minutes. After the first volley of stones hurled by the Spivs, the guards had scuttled away, some carrying a bar of bullion for a keepsake or for future use.

A week after the ray hit London, the city was an armed camp, divided between three groupings, the government officials, known loosely as "the Nobs," the Spivs, and the Reds.

The Nobs and the Spivs had a certain amount in common. Both groups had realized quickly the importance of gold long before the Reds. And they were much more alive to their own interests than the vast majority of Londoners, already pulling in their belts and pelting the few surviving cats and dogs with stones.

For the first three days, the Nobs fought several intense battles with the Spivs.

Of course the Spivs were dirty fighters, and there were more of them. They also tended to be younger. But they didn't stick together as well as the Nobs. The spirit of the Old School and the esprit de corps of the regimental mess slowly triumphed.

After three days of bloodshed—raid and counter-raid in and out of the alleys of the half-demolished city—a large number of the Spivs were ready to give up.

Many of them had asked the same question: "What are we going to get out of this? After all, you can't eat gold. What good is it?"

"You could make suits of armor," one Spiv had commented.

"Suits of armor?" another cried. "Is that what we're fighting for—suits of armor?"

The phrase, "suits of armor," was mockingly repeated around the stronghold of the Spivs, and it did more than anything else to bring about the deal made later with the Nobs. No reprisals, no victimization. Those who wanted to could go off on their own for a little quiet looting. Those who still wished to fight could join up with the Nobs and take up a common cause against the Reds.

And yet, golden suits of armor, together with golden swords, spears and other weapons, were the military key to the situation.

The Nobs realized that. They transported the gold from the vaults of the Bank to the Tower of London, for safekeeping. Then sent out Spivs to recruit a few blacksmiths from the ship-repair yards of the East End. They also commandeered a quantity of coal.

In a few days, forges were going in the Tower. Blocks of bullion formed anvils. Hammers of gold gave point and edge to spear-blades. Off course, gold is too malleable to take a real edge. But as weapons they were greatly superior to sticks or clubs.

Fortescue, to give his little army style, had gold breastplates and helmets made for himself and his staff. (Actually, when it came to a battle, that proved to be a bad move. The protection given by the armor was outweighed by the fact that leaders, glinting in the sun, could be so clearly picked out.)

The Spivs, who had gone out to find blacksmiths, reported back that in the East End the Reds were organizing. This terrified a number of the Bishops and other officials.

Actually, the Spivs themselves realized it was to their advantage to get the war over, and share the pickings with the winning side. So they piled on the agony. To judge by their reports, anyone would have thought that Red Terror was rife in Hackney Wick and the Mile End Road.

What actually happened in the working class areas was much simpler. Just as the unions took over the markets, so in the little streets whatever committees happened to be around took over the functions of government. In one street it might be the "darts committee" from the local pub, on another street it might be the committee that organized the annual outing to Southend. People who had been "toughing it" in their everyday lives tended to cling together in this crisis, too. Their experience in handling the hard times of life came in useful.

Not just thousands, but actually millions, of people needed to be fed. The small houses of the East End, having less metal in their structure, suffered less than the City or the West End, but the situation was quite grim everywhere.

As an emergency measure, neighbors began to make one or two fires in a street, burning woodwork and gathering around it cooperatively. But that wouldn't last forever. Such milk and food as remained was shared among the neediest cases. The small boys went out to hunt cats and dogs. Even rats were eaten.

Some bad times were experienced in the neighborhood of Regent's Park. And of course, the animals at the Zoo escaped from their cages the moment that the ray did its work. In the following days, the people in North London counted themselves lucky if they could catch a deer, or even a baboon. Half Hampstead lived off an elephant, which was chased with ropes across the Heath after wandering at large for a week. It was finally drowned in an ornamental fishpond.

But the escaped lions and tigers were the menace.

They headed East and South, owing to some mysterious instinct—and they were hungry. A tiger raided a butcher's shop in the Old Kent Road, and when courageously driven off by some local women with broomsticks, it lay in wait outside an orphanage and killed one of the inmates.

Worse things were to come, though.

Though few dared to speak of it, cannibalism was a growing concern. Anything vaguely suggesting it must be stamped out. London, like all great cities, contained human savages who might—when hungry enough—be tempted to prey on their own kind.

So volunteers were called in for Old Kent Road, and word was passed around, eventually reaching as far east as Greenwich, that these wild beasts and man-beasts must be firmly dealt with.

It was, in fact, the struggle to deal with the danger from these wild beasts, that gave the Reds their first all-London organization—which met in what had formerly been the offices of the Animal-Lovers' League in Battersea.

A hungry tiger is not easy to deal with.

They went for him with sticks—but one blow of his paw could splinter a stick and crush the man who held it.

They tried ropes, and managed to get the tiger rather tangled up. But the tiger was much less clumsy than the elephant caught at Hampstead. He soon wriggled free.

Finally, they borrowed a safety net from a gymnasium, and managed to enmesh the beast. Then they hauled it over the branch of a plane tree, and bombarded it with old bricks until its struggles ended.

The Reds—at their headquarters in Battersea—knew that the Nobs were wasting little time on rationing the available food, hunting down the escaped wild animals, or dealing with refugees. They knew that the production of arms from the one available metal—gold—was going on at great speed in the Tower of London. Soon they would be faced with a threat of armed force, imposing government on their good-natured anarchy.

But still they did nothing.

They were far too busy trying to get the hospitals and schools opened, burying the dead in temporary graveyards on bombsites, picketing food stores and other activities of a useful nature. In fact, the term Red that was applied to them, was merely a term of abuse, which they indignantly rejected. They were nothing but good-tempered members of darts matches and football club committees, and committees of workingmen's clubs and chapels, trying to get to grips with a problem that could not be solved, either by force or by good nature, but only by a miracle.

Charlie Smith, Chairman of the All-London Federation of Welfare Committees—or, as the Nobs referred to him, the leader of the Reds—had regretfully decided that he would have to organize an army, when Fis and Da landed on the shores of Britain.

CHAPTER FIVE
The Battle of London

FIS had been most enthusiastic about modifying the Annihilator so that it would wipe out all the metal of a hemisphere. But he had overlooked one thing. Barring a miracle he would also wipe out the airplane in which he and Da were travelling.

They were actually within sight of the white cliffs of Old England, flying at only a couple of hundred feet above sea level, when he pressed the fatal trigger.

They dropped like a couple of stones into fifty feet of cold, wet English Channel.

Hitting the water was a nasty smack. Fortunately, Fis had the physics of the situation clearly calculated and had presence of mind enough to enter the sea feet first, so as to reduce the area of impact.

But he went down such a long way that the nasty saline stuff—a modified form of that combination of oxygen and hydrogen known as "water," was beginning to be forced into his lungs. Then, after several seemingly endless moments, he started to rise once more. He looked around desperately for Da.

She was nowhere to be seen!

Just as panic was beginning to grip at his heart, she broke through the surface, tossed back her hair and grinned, like someone who had merely jumped off a diving board.

"This stuff," she spluttered, "isn't as buoyant as on Mars."

He swam toward her, delighted. Then realized that a catastrophe had occurred.

"I dropped the Annihilator!" he gasped.

Da's eyes widened at this and she put her hand to her mouth to suppress a cry of surprise.

"It must be somewhere down at the bottom of the sea." Fis continued.

But the surprised expression on Da's face quickly returned to normal. She turned on her side and struck out for the shore.

"A good place for it, too," she answered calmly over her shoulder.

By the time they reached the strip of sand beneath the chalk cliffs they were nearly exhausted. There was a gap in the cliffs where a footpath wound. Wearily they climbed up.

"London," said Fis, "is somewhere north of here."

"I'm hungry," Da reminded him.

"So are most of the other inhabitants of England," he retorted.

They are vegetarian on Mars—that goes without saying. But after having sampled grass, unripe wheat, and green fruit (and been chased by a farmer with a whip in his hand) Fis was ready to eat almost anything.

He caught a rabbit in a snare made of small willow branches. Da couldn't bear to see him kill, gut, and skin it. She concentrated on trying to make a fire by friction in order to cook the rabbit meat. But it wasn't as easy in practice as it looked in the textbooks of archaeology. Finally, she got a flickering flame going, and they tried to grill the skinned rabbit, which looked pathetic and sanguinary.

They were so hungry that they ate it—nearly raw—and enjoyed it. Da expected to hate every mouthful, but she found herself sucking the very bones.

"I wonder if this will do something to me?" she asked. Fis raised his eyebrows. "I wonder if eating this dead animal, this corpse, will make me like the Earth people—jealous, and cruel, and selfish?"

"It's not their diet," Fis assured her. "It's their brain. They can't Overthink like we can."

"I wonder," she answered, licking her fingers one by one.

Sixty miles by aircraft is a journey of a few minutes. Sixty miles on foot, heading for London from the coast is three days' walking under good conditions. Under conditions where you have to trap your food, and steer clear of desperate refugees, it's a hopeless journey across a savage land.

Walking across the North Downs they came across something that gave Fis pause to think. There was a quarry in the chalk hillside. Nearby were the ruins of what had once been a limekiln.

An old man was squatting down beside a pile of flints. Next to him were a couple of young men. At first, Fis took them to be Americans. They wore ties with pretty women painted on them and suits with exaggerated shoulders. They had their hair cut in the fashion common to American college boys and English convicts. But their pinched and pale faces were those of a pair of rather ill-at-ease young men, trying to carry out the old adage: "If you feel scared, wear a big hat."

They were English all right. Fis overheard one say to the old man: "I ain't ever seen nuffink so 'orrible slow as you, guvnor."

Seeing Da's puzzled expression, Fis silently Overthought the remark that this was an English dialect, known as Cockney.

The other young man said, "I'll crahn yer if yer down't gi' a move on." And he threateningly shook a stick that he was carrying.

But the old, wizened man, with the complexion of an ancient apple, kept on with his work at the same slow pace.

Then Fis realized what the old man was doing.

"It's the Stone Age, all over again," he Overthought. And that was precisely true.

The old man was probably one of the last of the flint-makers left in England. And he was painstakingly knocking slivers off flints—sharper even than blades of gold. The most effective things for weapons that existed in the whole of Britain.

The Nobs and the Spivs combined were sharp-witted. These young men were one of their scouting parties, sent out from London to gather in supplies of flints for the coming battles with the Reds.

Just then there was a shout of defiance from the further edge of the quarry. The two overdressed young men looked up, rose to their feet, and waved their sticks threateningly.

And then they fell, suddenly, sadly, like a pair of grotesque Goliaths. A moment later, with grins on their faces, three other men walked down the quarry side.

They had flat caps and the hands of people used to honest work—large, knotted and skilful. And in each right hand dangled a slingshot.

The supplies of rubber remaining in the shops had been confiscated by the Reds. Every haberdasher's in London had been looted of its elastic.

"Reckon you'd had enough of those two, dad," said the man walking out front, who appeared to be the leader.

"Reckon I had."

"I'm Joe Smith. My brother, Charlie, is Chairman of the All-London Federation of Welfare Committees—the chaps they call the Reds."

"My name's Tom," said the flint-knapper. "I 'aven't voted for anyone since Lloyd George's day. And what puzzles me is—what am I going to do with all these flints?"

Joe Smith looked down at the pile of sharpened stones while his companions, in the loose rubble at the foot of the quarry, started to scratch a rough grave for the two dead Spivs.

Joe picked up a flint, tried it on his thumb.

"Sharp as a knife," he said, thoughtfully.

"That's right."

"Anyone else besides you know how to take splinters off these flints?"

"I did hear tell there was a chap one time of day down in Dorset, but I dare say he's died."

Joe scratched his chin. He wasn't as bright as his brother Charlie, but he was bright enough to put two and two together.

"Could you teach me and my mates how to do it?"

"Glad to," said the old chap. "I never found anyone with enough patience, except one young chap, and he was killed in the War."

Joe turned around and said, "Alf—you gotta pinch a horse an' ride like heck to tell Charlie about this. We got something here better than the Nobs' gold. Tell him to send out carriers and bring in loads of flints. I'll teach the knack of doing it to the boys—"

"I getcha," said Alf, who then waddled off on bowlegs to hunt down a horse. It was a long cry from riding in Selling Plates to cantering on a brewer's dray up the Dover Road. But Alf could see the point about the flints, too.

Da and Fis, dodging Reds and Spivs alike, once more headed north.

"You see," Fis said, thinking aloud, "already certain groupings are emerging, in this country, at least. Of course, Britain is especially civilized, but the same thing will be happening in other parts of the world. Those overdressed young men—I wouldn't have confidence in their ability to prevail. No one with real self-confidence would doll himself up in such a fashion. And they acted like bullies."

"Bullies?" she queried.

"Someone who imposes his will an another, by force," he explained.

"But these men in flat caps—they seem to have imagination. They appear able to see broad possibilities. Take their catapults—or slingshots I believe they call them here on Earth—for instance. Only the lower classes are skilled in the use of catapults—they are a popular weapon with small boys of the working class. And a skill like that is retained into manhood. So that grouping, when it comes to a fight, will have formidable fire-power…"

"And is that important?" asked Da, innocently.

"My dear," he answered, "haven't you ever made a study of war?"

"I had a fairy-story book which mentioned it," she said, "when I was a little girl. But my mother said it was horrid, and took it away from me."

The first real clash between the two armies took place in Trafalgar Square. The Square wasn't, on the face of it, much changed by the destructive effects of the ray. Nelson's column was still standing, although the metal statues had gone. The windows of the shops had no glass. Charing Cross Station was a shell. Refugees from blocks of London County Council flats built on steel frameworks were camping in the National Gallery. At night, to keep warm, they wrapped themselves in priceless canvasses. By day they lit their fires with books from the second-hand bookshops in nearby Charing Cross Road.

It was those refugees that caused the trouble.

Charlie Smith's advanced posts at Billingsgate and Leadenhall markets (now completely empty of food) reported that the Nobs and Spivs were proceeding out of the Tower, and marching in full battle array West, to push the Reds' stronghold out of Battersea and back into the East End proper.

They even had cavalry—composed of a few mounts from the Life-guards, the polo ponies from Hurlingham, and a couple of horses that at one time had belonged to the mounted police.

The Reds' army was composed of a solid mass of men with slingshots, and some who were experimenting with bows and arrows. One or two of them were inclined to jeer when they heard of the cavalry that was soon to confront them, but Charlie Smith himself was worried. Could his men withstand a cavalry charge?

So, having selected Trafalgar Square as the best battleground, he drew up a battle plan. The line of advance, if he won the battle, would be along the Strand, to smash the Nobs' stronghold in the City of London and cut off the City from Mayfair and Belgravia. Line of retreat would be through St. James's Park to the river, and then across the pontoon bridge, which his engineers had constructed, made of timber from Thames' barges, lashed together with rope.

Charlie sent an advanced guard of his most skilled slingshot marksmen to seize the National Gallery. There, high up, protected by the parapet and with a clear range right across the Square, they could enfilade the Nobs and Spivs when they arrived.

But in Fortesque, leader of the Nobs, Charlie was up against a trained military man who knew every trick of the game.

Fortescue sent an advance guard of his own, a detachment of cavalry and some men with spears and short swords hammered of gold, right around the Red outpost in Covent Garden. This advance party entered the Square via St. Martin's Lane.

Now, if the flanking slingshotsmen sent to the National Gallery had been wide-awake, this would have been their chance.

But it didn't work out that way.

When they saw the body of determined-looking men approach, the squatters in the National Gallery, who felt a bit guilty about their destruction of paintings, got ready to fight for their temporary home.

Admittedly, the squatters had only stones, rubbish, and the contents of slop-buckets to throw, but they were protected by the steps and the parapet. And they started their resistance a few moments before the Nobs' outflanking party, down St. Martin's Lane, entered the Square.

Had the leaders of the advance guard of slingshotsmen known their business, they would have gone forward to parley with the squatters, promised them protection, and granted them a future right to the Gallery. He would have painted the Nobs as people coming to dispossess them and so won the squatters as allies. But he was hot-blooded, and spoiling for a fight. So he missed his chance of enfilading the Nobs' advance guard because they instead engaged in a squabble with a mob of enraged and apprehensive women.

The party Fortescue had—with shrewd foresight—sent via St. Martin's Lane took the Reds' main body fairly in the flank.

It was a strange sight. The cavalry comprised a few guards' officers, with no buttons on their uniforms. Also mounted was a city gent who happened to be in formal morning dress the day the ray struck, and so was now mounted wearing a gray cutaway coat and a battered topper. In the riders' ranks was also a sprinkling of "men about town," still riding with crumpled elegance and armed with golden lances that glittered in the sunshine.

Behind came the infantry—a mixture of Spiv bruisers and young army officers from the Junior Army and Navy Club, and the Royal Naval College at Greenwich (these latter heroes had swum the Thames at the Isle of Dogs in order to join the Nobs' resistance). They had short golden stabbing swords in the front rank, and six-foot spears in the rear rank.

Fortesque was leading the main party. He had put in command of his flank foray a dashing young army officer, Peveril, who had won the Grand National as an amateur several years before.

As badge of his rank, Peveril wore a breastplate of solid gold and gold greaves on his thighs. His helmet similarly gleamed and glittered but was so heavy it literally made thought difficult.

Peveril saw the drab-suited foot soldiers of the Reds' army emerge through the Admiralty Arch.

With a gay hunting "Tallyho!" he led the Gentlemen of England in a full-tilt charge across the Square.

A concentrated volley from the steps of the Gallery would have waylaid to his charge, but the squabble with the squatters there was in full tilt.

At a glance, Charlie Smith took in the situation, and shouted orders to the front rank of his slingshotsmen. The volley was well aimed. Peveril, an unmistakable target, was toppled over like a ninepin, and his glorious golden armor hit the paving stones with a clang.

But a shower of stones isn't enough to halt a cavalry charge. A few horses stumbled, but the bulk hurtled onward, an irresistible mass.

Then one of the leading slingshotsmen had an inspiration.

As well as small stones, he had raided a couple of deserted toyshops in Lambeth and taken all their marbles and small glass toys for his slingshot.

When the cavalry was fifteen yards away, just as his comrades to right and left were beginning to waver, he took a handful of these marbles and scattered them across the roadway.

It was cruel, but effective.

Those Hurlingham ponies, for instance, could have kept their footing on the most slippery grass, but let one hoof touch a marble, and they were helpless. They skidded and collapsed, precipitating their riders to the ground.

The cavalry charge, which might have ended in disaster for the Reds, turned into a confused melee. Fists were flailing, golden weapons flashed.

Then the main party of the Spivs' and Nobs' army, coming down the Strand, began to enter the Square. The Reds were confused and had broken rank—and some of their number had been killed or wounded by stabs at short range.

But the main army of the Nobs was intact, fresh, marching with rank upon serried rank of glittering weapons.

The Reds didn't need Charlie Smith to tell them they should grab the swords and spears of the fallen enemy. The weakness of an army composed almost entirely of slingshotsmen had been made evident. Once an enemy swordsman could get to stabbing range, the slingshotsmen was at his mercy.

Making a snap decision, Charlie decided on a fighting retreat.

In the front rank were men who had seized the long cavalry spears or the dropped swords of the flank attack that had been led by Peveril.

Behind them were the slingshotsmen.

The men with spears were to act as rearguard.

They still talk in London of that fighting retreat across St. James's Park and through Victoria to the river. What seemed at the time so timid as almost to appear cowardly, proved a brilliant stroke.

Again and again the Nobs and Spivs attacked. Thundering cavalry charges were met by handfuls of marbles, and the spiky resistance of lances held firmly by two or three determined men on each shaft. Infantry attacks were disseminated by catapult volleys at long range, and then broken up by cut and thrust.

Every Nob or Spiv who fell meant another gold spear or stabbing-sword for the Reds, multiplying their bristling weapons, which made their line seem so formidable, to the attackers.

The Nobs and Spivs couldn't believe they were not winning. They had contempt for their enemy—had he not been foolish enough to let the gold reserves of the Bank fall into their hands? And they seemed to be pushing the Reds back—past Buckingham Palace, past the ruins of the Victoria bus station.

But every time they attacked, they lost two men for every dead Red. And the Reds had considerably outnumbered them from the start.

Then they reached the riverbank.

There were murmurings, particularly from the businessmen and politicians among the Nobs, against Fortescue's leadership. The young officers were more used to discipline—but even they were beginning to wonder at the wisdom of a strategy that wore down their numbers in order to take territory which couldn't be held.

Fortescue was in the position of a general who needed a success to retrieve his reputation.

And there, before him was the pontoon bridge. The only link between London North and South. The key to these flank raids from South London by the Reds.

If he could capture that bridge and destroy it, he would be able to claim success.

He ordered his dispirited cavalry to mobilize for a new charge.

But Charlie Smith, too, could see the strategic importance of the bridge. Trenches had already been dug to cover the bridgehead on the North side.

Looking down on them, Fortescue could see that the trenches around the bridgehead bristled like a hedgehog with spearsmen and slingshotsmen. He knew in his heart of hearts that capturing the bridge could only occur by a miracle. But keeping a stiff upper lip, he turned to his men, and spoke them words of encouragement, reminding them of their old schools, their service in Empire, Government and Commerce, their wives and families down in Surrey, who would remain for ever proud of those who died a hero's death.

Looking down on the vital pontoon bridge, maybe the hearts of the Gentlemen, the Nobs, began to glow with warmth and pride. But the hearts of the Spivs began to sink. Because already the bulk of the Reds' army had crossed and were heading for the security of Battersea Park.

A few young officers cheered as Nobs and Spivs made their final attack. But it was a feeble cheer.

The issue was never in doubt.

The men in the bridgehead, unless they could be starved out, could never be dislodged.

But every attack would cost the Nobs and Spivs dearly.

Fortescue charged three times. Each time they pressed home their attack with desperate fervor. Unless dislodged and driven from power, the mob, through sheer numbers, would remorselessly and irresistibly conquer London. And London was the key to England. It would mean an end to civilization as the Nobs and Spivs knew it.

Yet after each charge they had to withdraw, leaving men dead upon the field.

Yet their discipline held. Fortescue, before the attack, had ordered that none of their vital, irreplaceable weapons were to fall into enemy hands. And he was being obeyed. But the significant sight was the number of Nobs and Spivs who were carrying two, or even three, weapons retrieved from fallen comrades.

After the third attack, the Spivs mutinied.

"Use your loaf," said Gus, their leader, "why not swim down the river at night, and set the darn bridge afire?"

"Very well, then," said Fortescue, briskly. "Do I take it you are volunteering?"

"I never learned to swim," said Gus, promptly.

And Fortescue, who was no fool, realized that the Spivs had had enough of being heroes. Wisely, he withdrew the remainder of his force, and returned, via Pimlico and Bayswater, to the Nobs' advance post in the West End.

The Nobs had neither won nor lost—they had merely taught the Reds a lesson—that even numbers backed up by slingshotsmen couldn't win, without cavalry and edged weapons.

As the enemy force drew off, Charlie Smith crossed the pontoon bridge, leaving a subaltern in charge of the bridgehead force.

He was deeply thoughtful.

The Nobs and Spivs would, of course, now be preparing their own catapults... And although a certain number of the gold weapons had been captured, the Nobs still had a monopoly of metal.

Cavalry, too, was going to be important.

He racked his brains. He was worried—so preoccupied that he hardly bothered to look up when a sentry reported that his brother Joe was coming in, with a pack-column and two prisoners.

The prisoners were Fis and Da.

They had traveled north from the flint quarry. Near the outskirts of London they ran into trouble from the rival bands of refugees who were flooding into the country in search of food. Farmers opposing them were banding together to keep a hold on their crops.

This guerilla warfare was going on around the edges of every big town.

After a few days of hunger, the city people who hadn't become involved in the Civil War, or who lived outside an area where the Reds' rationing system was functioning, started trekking into the country.

A pitched battle was fought on the Chilterns between rustlers seeking sheep to take and slaughter, and farmers protecting their flocks. The farmers, being in a permanent minority, started using terror tactics, trying to intimidate their enemy. They hung rustlers from the boughs of Burnham Beeches, decorated with warning placards. They organized regular patrols, and threatened poachers with branding. But they lost out more often than they won.

Food, which might have saved many lives if rationed, was either used by rustlers to glut themselves in a quick meal, or else hidden by farmers.

Fis and Da ran into trouble at a chicken farm in North Kent.

The chicken farmer had already fought a pitched battle against refugees heading southeast from Croydon. This time he had won. Then local people had come to him, begging for eggs, or even chickens. He laughed when they offered pound notes. He had started a bartering price list, the items on which continually went higher in value—until after a few days an egg cost a remarkable amount in bartered goods. The chicken farmer's customers needed to buy or else face starvation. And so he traded at exorbitant prices for things that were priceless, now that the wheels of industry had stopped forever.

There were, of course, risks. One night the farmer lost four birds to rustlers, so the next night he made preparations to trap the thieves, should they return. He left a suckling pig beneath an apple tree with a large net concealed in the branches above. He lay in wait with the big net ready to trap any intruders.

On Mars, the sense of property isn't very well developed the way it is on Earth. No one would think of complaining if someone lacking food took some from another Martian possessing more than he needed. So it was pardonable for Da and Fis, seeing the sucking pig apparently left out beneath the apple tree, to think of taking it for themselves.

The owner of the pig, hidden in the leafage of the tree, waited until the pair was pursuing the pig around the base of the tree. Then he dropped the net.

Fis and Da felt, quite literally, like trapped fish.

The owner of the pig had thought his plan out carefully. He had placed a wooden pulley from a branch of the fruit tree. As the pair enmeshed themselves by their struggles, he dropped to the ground, caught the rope that dangled from the pulley and hauled hard.

Helpless, the two Martians were jerked into the air.

Fis and Da appreciated each other's company, but not at quite such close quarters. And Fis's blood began to boil as the man on the ground, having hauled them up so that they were helpless and swinging, commenced belaboring them with a thick stick.

They spun and whirled. There was nothing Fis could do to ensure that he got the lion's share of the blows except Overthinking encouraging sentiments to Da, who responded with the reflection that she was experiencing at least one emotion characteristic of Earth dwellers, namely…anger.

And it happened to be just then that Joe Smith and his pack train—men loaded with haversacks full of flints—trudged up the road adjacent to the farm.

"Pigs!" shouted one of Smith's men.

Fis knew that word was a term of abuse on Earth, besides being the name of the animal beneath them. He wondered whether these newcomers would prove friends or enemies.

"Chicken!" shouted another enthusiastic man just behind Smith.

"Don't touch the apples—they're not ripe!" Joe Smith warned. Joe looked intently at the strange spectacle under the tree—a man and girl, strung up in a net, swinging to and fro and being savagely beaten.

He shouted, "See if those are two of our people!"

The farmer did his best to defend himself with his stick, but he was soon overwhelmed. One of Smith's men then sawed through the rope with a sharp flint, and the two Martians hit earth with a collective thump. They painfully got to their feet, and disentangled themselves.

"Coo, what a smasher!" someone exclaimed, his eyes staring intently on Da's lovely figure. Even bruised and disheveled, Da was a beauty by Earth standards.

"What are you," Joe asked sternly, "a Red, a Spiv or a Nob?"

"I'm strictly neutral," Fis answered.

"You talk like a City man," Joe said, suspiciously. "I dare say you're a Nob, and ashamed to admit it."

"I'm definitely not a Nob. But I'm not a Red or a Spiv, either. I'm just an observer."

"Are you an Englishman?"

"No."

"You talk very good English. Let's look at your hands."

Martians' hands are quite like a human's, except that the little finger is as long as the ring finger.

"Funny-looking hands. You never done no hard work, though, I can tell that. Let's look at yours, Miss. You've got the same odd little fingers—you brother and sister?"

"No," said Fis, boldly. "You might call us man and wife. We're on our honeymoon."

"I daresay that accounts for your being strictly neutral. Well—are you worth taking prisoner…I wonder? We feed our prisoners so they have to work. What can you do?"

"Oh, he can do practically anything," Da replied in a confident tone.

Joe Smith asked, "Can you do anything in the flint chipping line?"

"I've made a special study of the Stone Age," Fis told him. And though this was true, not a soul believed him.

"Can you make—now let me see—can you make a saw from flint?" asked Joe, picking on the hardest thing he could think of.

"I can show you how they made their saws in Stone Age times," Fis said. "I'll make you a saw of the type most popular with the Aztecs and the Ancient Egyptians."

When Smith nodded, Fis knew he was going to be put to the test. First he got a long, straight stick. Then with the aid of one of the flints, which had already been cut, he sliced a groove along in it. With infinite adroitness, he started to chip minute sharp fragments of flint, each roughly the shape of a saw-tooth. These he wedged into the groove, gripping them tight by binding the stick with string from the net.

The suspicious stares on the faces of Smith and his men turned rapidly to stares of admiration as they squatted around and watched Fis work on the flint. Smith's men were skilled workers themselves, and they appreciated skill when they saw it. And the manual skill of Martians, even of brainworkers, is high by Earth standards.

"Gut is better than string," Fis said. "Now soak it in some liquid such as water, so that it shrinks and holds the teeth tightly."

Joe took Fis' Stone Age saw in his hand and approached the apple tree. He reached up toward a dead bough and gingerly made a couple of strokes with the saw.

"It works…" he said softly.

"Of course it works," said Fis. "The human race had no better tool for tens of thousands of years."

Joe turned around and faced the men. Being brother to the Chief, he had a broader view of the problems facing England than others did. "Boys," he said, "we've got a future. Not much of a one. But some."

"Can you make any other tools?" asked a skeptic.

"Sickles are made on the same principle. Axe heads, knife blades—"

"Swords and spears?"

"If you're going to waste your time and effort in anything as wasteful as fighting—yes."

And all the way from the chicken farm to Battersea Fis and Da were guarded as carefully as a couple of valuable, highly trained performing animals.

CHAPTER SIX
The Flint Factory

"IMPORTANT prisoners you may be," Charlie Smith was saying, "but you talk like Nobs. I'd like to hear you account for yourselves."

He was sitting outside his tent in Battersea Park, looking over some papers and marking them with a quill pen.

On the turf his troops were drilling. While the Golden Pike men went through their exercises, men with stabbing swords engaged in mock combat. The Red bowmen, using flint-tipped arrows, were practicing at targets that had formerly been statues, erected at public expense in the Gardens by the London County Council.

"So you're getting ready for war," Fis said, looking around him. "You can't go much longer living on what survives from the past—the food, the clothes. Sooner or later you've got to start working constructively—planting crops, weaving cloth—"

"I know that full well," said Charlie Smith. "But this war's been forced upon us. Just let me deal with the Nobs and their Spiv allies and I'll lead my people out of London and settle them in the countryside. Then they will be able to lead constructive lives—"

"But won't that mean another war...against the country people?"

"It will," said Charlie, promptly, "and we're bound to win it because we've got the numbers, the weapons, and, above all, the organized discipline."

To Fis it sounded just like human history repeating itself.

"And you can't think of any prospect, but one war after another?"

"Can you?"

"Why not go and talk things over with the Nobs and Spivs, come to some arrangement with them…"

Charlie laid down his quill pen carefully (it had come from one of the swans on the pond, which had long since been slaughtered for food).

"So that's what you are—one of these people who doesn't understand realities here on earth. You must have spent all your life up in the clouds—"

"That's perfectly true," said Da, boldly. "We neither of us belong to this world at all."

"If you want to go and talk to the leaders of the Nobs and Spivs, I'll let you go freely. And if afterwards you want to come back here, that's O.K., too. But first, you can spend a little while teaching my people how to make tools of flints. And when you go, to avoid treachery, I'll keep your wife here as a hostage. Now don't get alarmed. We don't ill-treat women on this side—it's our enemies who have a monopoly on that…"

"I'll show you how to make the implements of peace," said Fis, "sickles, hoes, axes."

"That's fair enough," said Charlie Smith, "we shall need those, too, eventually. The spears and arrowheads we shall learn to make for ourselves."

Da and Fis stood silent, for a moment. To the onlookers, they might have been praying or engaged in a daydream. Actually they were Overthinking rapidly.

Da had an intuitive feeling that these strange working men could be trusted. She Overthought her confidence in them, and finally persuaded Fis to let her stay.

Fis set off across the pontoon bridge, a solitary figure, unharmed, bearing a safe-conduct to see him through the Reds' lines.

Fortescue sat in state in the Tower of London, one of the celebrated ravens perched on his wrist. He was in his own golden armor, and looked like a figure from the Middle Ages. Behind him stood his horse, harnessed with a golden bit and held by a spearman of his army.

He took the safe-conduct from Fis, and read it. "So they kept your wife as hostage?"

"That's so."

"Pretty tough, old boy. I hear they treat women darned badly on the other side. There have been all sorts of rumors about heiresses used as washerwomen—darned disgraceful. Makes our fellows' blood boil."

"The other side says much the same things about you."

"Impudent lackeys!" Fortescue replied with immense sincerity.

Fis couldn't help liking the man. On Mars, with that force and drive, he might have ended up an Elected Global Brain. But he was handicapped by a most un-Martian hatred for the common run of his fellows.

"You seem pretty much the right sort yourself," Fortescue remarked. "I won't ask questions; we're very democratic over here. Got several fellas in my army that would never get into my Club. And the Spivs are a rum lot—but good-hearted chaps all of them, though we see that they keep their distance. You've shown the right sort of nerve in coming here to join us, leaving the love of your life with those rascals. Tell you what I'll do—I can't make you an officer right away, too many of 'em already. But I'll put you up for the cavalry."

"I didn't come here to volunteer."

"How do you expect to rescue your lady fair unless our next offensive is successful?"

"By removing all need for an offensive. The chaps on the other side have mastered the art of making tools from flint…"

"Flint, eh? That's a good tip. Any little piece of information like that is a great help in planning strategy…"

"Try to forget strategy for a moment. Look, here's London. I suppose about five or six million of the original inhabitants must be left. Most of them are starving. They back you up or else the chaps across the river, because in the army they have a hope of sharing in what food there is left. Now why waste your time in fighting, when to avoid starvation so much needs doing—planting, rationing supplies, building up fuel stocks ready for the winter…"

Fortescue had a superior grin on his face. In fact had Fis not been a Martian born and bred he would have felt rather like knocking the expression off with a blow from his fist.

"So you're a sky-pilot, eh? I knew from the start there was something not quite right about you. All this brotherly love stuff. Now listen to me. First it was the Reds that wiped out all metal—I saw a confidential report from the Suez Canal Zone, long before the trouble reached these islands, putting it down to a mysterious submarine in the Red Sea. And the very moment the metal went, the Reds started taking over the markets and other key positions. They were using the national crisis to promote a revolution. Well…the chaps under my command are not going to let them get away with it. The whole world can't be in the same position as these islands. Somewhere civilization must be surviving—someday help is going to arrive. And so my chaps and I here, in the grand old Tower of London, where so much history was made, are going to stick it out to the end—knowing that every day we hang on brings rescue nearer—"

A crowd of his men had gathered around as Fortescue spoke. There was a murmur of applause and agreement.

"And you absolutely believe that?" Fis asked.

"Absolutely."

"If I gave you complete proof that you were mistaken about the Russian submarine, what would you say?"

"'I should say you were the dupe of Red propaganda."

"And there's absolutely no chance of parleying with the leader of the Reds over the practical jobs that need to be done?"

"Absolutely none."

"Then there's no purpose served in my staying here. I'd better be getting back to my wife in Battersea Park."

The smile went from Fortescue's face. At a hand gesture, a couple of Spivs seized Fis in a grip that they had practiced when working as chuckers out at a wrestling booth.

"You're mistaken there," said Fortescue. "You've seen my fortifications in the City, my new secret weapons, my methods for training the troops. I certainly don't propose to let you go."

Fis felt his heart sink. Da a prisoner in one camp, himself a prisoner in the other, and all because he mistakenly thought that the Earth creatures would respond to an appeal to reason.

"And we'll drag out of you the truth about yourself," Fortescue was saying. "There are ways and means of making men talk that were kept in this Tower as survivals of a bygone age. Before the night is out, you'll be regretting that our ancestors made the Rack out of leather and wood, without a scrap of metal in its composition…"

And with this threat ringing in his ears, Fis was led off to the Bloody Tower.

The Tower of London looked quite different from the ancient building over which parties of schoolchildren used to trail in far-off days, scattering orange peels and gasping at the Crown Jewels. The gold from the Crown Jewels had long since been hammered into broadswords, and the gems themselves put on one side to serve as medals, to reward gallantry in battle, with the Koh-i-noor serving as the V.C.

The huge masonry walls were still erect, making the Tower the strongest fortress in the City of London.

Looking out through a slit in his cell in the Bloody Tower, which at one time had housed Sir Walter Raleigh and Mary, Queen of Scots, Fis watched the Nob soldiers drill.

The door opened. A young Spiv, wearing a suit with padded shoulders, stood in the doorway.

"Interested, I see," said the Spiv.

"Mildly."

"They said you was a spy."

"They said wrong."

"Garn—you can trust me. I saw you watching the new tactics. Tactics? They make you weep. It's nuffink but drill, drill, drill until yer aching feet falls off."

He pushed a plate of food across the cell. So far as Fis could see, the meat was that of a rat, which had died a natural death before being skinned and dressed for the table.

"And now they've made you cook?"

"S'right. Cor, what a lark. Nuffink but grumble, grumble, grumble, orl day long. Is it right what they say bout the Reds?"

"What is it they say?"

"That they smoke cigars all day, an' loot the houses of the rich?"

This Spiv, Fis reflected, couldn't Overthink and discover he was lying.

"That's the least of it," he answered.

"An' they have duchesses to empty the slops? An' beautiful society women to clean their boots'?"

Evidently this Spiv had taken Fortescue's line in war propaganda much too seriously.

"Hundreds of beautiful women—" said Fis.

"And deserters'?"

"All the most beautiful women are reserved for deserters. A tent full of film actresses and debutantes, and no holds barred—"

"What do I do? How do I—"

"You just turn around," said Fis, gently, persuasively, noting that the Spiv had left the door ajar, and that the platter on which the dead rat had been borne was of heavy stoneware.

Fis put a bit too much strength into the blow. As he stepped through the door he wondered vaguely whether that crunching noise had been stoneware or skull. But he had presence of mind enough to stoop for the gold sword that his guard had borne.

For one thing, another gold sword would be useful to the Reds.

For another thing, possession of a gold sword was as good as a certificate of exemplary behavior, signed by Fortescue himself. Only trained soldiers had gold swords.

And so it proved.

Fis walked down the steps of the Bloody Tower, and no one challenged him. He was a tall, aristocratic-looking chap, carrying a gold sword. Obviously a Nob.

He got to the parapet without being challenged. He looked up and down river. And there he saw Fortescue's secret weapon.

Amazing. He couldn't believe his eyes.

When the Annihilator ray struck, nearly all the shipping in the water—being made of metal—simply vanished, leaving flotsam varying from a few articles of furniture to entire cargoes.

The few wooden ships—like the Cutty Sark—took a little longer to disintegrate. Their copper sheathing went, then the bolts, the nails and the other metalwork holding together vital parts of their timbers vanished. The strain started to show. The timber ships slowly fell apart.

However, anchored below the place once occupied by Tower Bridge, was a small schooner-rigged sailing vessel, covered with Fortescue's workmen, who were rapidly carrying out alterations and repairs.

On her stern Fis could read:

SILVA
Magnetic Survey Ship, London

Then Fis remembered.

Radar on Earth was still at a primitive stage. Most ships still navigated by the "compass"—a suspended magnet, which turned toward the magnetic North. But in metal ships, special allowance had to be made for the deviations caused by nearby masses of iron and steel, and no compass was reliable until this had been done.

To do research into compasses and the magnetic pole, a vessel was needed with a minimum of metal in it. And that was the *Silva*.

A few copper nails, maybe, would need replacing. And there were Fortescue's artificers, replacing copper by wooden or golden pegs. Such a vessel wouldn't survive an ocean voyage. But it would keep intact on the trip upstream, from the Tower to Battersea. It would smash a gap in the pontoon bridge. And it would serve as a floating platform, down from which troops could leap for an assault on the Red headquarters.

Tidal water had covered Tower Beach. Fis climbed on to the parapet, and was thrusting the sword into his belt, ready to dive, when he heard a shout behind him.

A squad of men was thundering toward him from the direction of Traitors' Gate. They all brandished swords.

Fis turned and made his dive.

As he broke through the surface of the water, he had a momentary glimpse of other men diving in after him.

A swift glance around showed Fis the ruined foundations of Tower Bridge, projecting like stumps from the river. He struck out for the farthest one.

And behind him came the ominous splash and gasp of trained swimmers approaching—closer and closer.

Fis struck out vigorously. His keen mind was swiftly taking in the physical facts of the situation. The state of the tide, the strength of the current. By heading a little upstream of the bridge foundations, he was able to hit them exactly.

He scrambled up, scraping his knees. Great lumps of masonry stood around his feet, left there from the moment when the great bridge was washed down in ruins, when the metal-cased hydraulic tanks vanished, and left hundreds of gallons of water to drop through masonry.

Fis looked back at his pursuers—there were four of them.

The leading swimmer was gripping a gold stabbing sword between his teeth. He had a huge moustache, too big even for the cavalry. He must have been an ex-R.A.F. pilot.

Fis picked up a large rock and threw. Standing above the swimmer, and having the advantage of superb Martian condition, he had no need for a second shot. The lump of stone, weighing many pounds, struck the moustached swimmer in the small of his back. He crumpled like a rabbit hit with buckshot.

Before the second man could swerve, a second huge stone was dropped on his skull with a sickening thud. He too sank, then bobbed up one final time, then sank for good.

The third and fourth men started treading water, just out of range. One actually had a monocle in his eye. The other, who sported a toothbrush moustache, shouted to the other something that Fis didn't catch. Then they turned and swam in opposite directions, one on each side of the massive lump of ruined masonry cropping up from the calm surface of the Thames.

By dividing their forces, they hoped that at least one would get ashore and come to grips with him.

These men were heroes—reckless—but heroes. No doubt they had been told to get the prisoner back at all costs. And "at all costs" evidently meant even at the cost of their lives.

He turned toward the man with the toothbrush moustache, moved around the foundation carrying a thirty-pound rock, then waited for a moment until the swimmer was coming in to land, and hurled.

There was no need for a second try. The man gasped when the rock hit him, and the river water was momentarily stained with blood.

Then from behind him, Fis heard a grunting gasp. And a man taller than himself, though less broad in the shoulder, ran forward, a monocle glinting in his eye, while a gold stabbing sword gleamed in his hand.

Fis grabbed for his own sword.

Fencing was a sport that died out on Mars eleven hundred years earlier—a fact Fis regretted at that moment.

The monocled man approached him, stabbing, thrusting, and parrying, with a mixture of science and fury. Fis backed away. Agonizingly the short gold blade gashed his left forearm. The pain almost made him drop his own weapon.

He backed away desperately, keeping his eyes glued on his antagonist stumbling over the tumbled rocks. On the face of the monocled man was a look expressive both of hatred and of delight. He was playing with Fis as a cat plays with a mouse—maneuvering him into position for the deathblow.

The best physique in the world couldn't stand against the pressure of that scientific onslaught. But suddenly Fis became aware of new noises, unfamiliar ones.

The dip and splash of oar strokes.

The scrape of iron-shod boots on rock.

And a calm, quiet voice, slightly Cockneyfied, which said: "You'd better both put up your hands."

Fis put his hands up obediently. But the Nob, hearing an accent similar to that of the despised Cockney, turned with a snarl, and stabbed out ferociously at the newcomer.

A sound was heard that had not been encountered since the ray struck and the civil war started—the brief, peremptory cough of a revolver.

The monocled Nob pitched face forward on the stones, and he too was dead as a stone.

Fis saw a man in a peaked cap, pistol in hand.

At the foot of the broken masonry was a ship's lifeboat, pulled by eight oarsmen. All white, all speaking that variety of Cockney.

And out in midstream was a two-thousand-ton tramp, smoke pouring from her dirty funnel, with the name *Manukua* painted on her bows, and the New Zealand flag flying from her jackstaff.

"London looks a mess," said Fis, in the friendliest tone he could contrive.

"Too right," said the ship's captain. "Now tell me, cobber, where do I find the Government?"

Fis smiled. "Give the Tower of London a wide berth. It's full of gangsters. If you want to find the Government you must sail upstream until you come to Battersea Park…"

The crewmembers of the tramp were all on deck, looking with bored expressions at the ruins of London.

They'd seen plenty of ruined cities—Buenos Aires, Rio, Galveston. Land, raid the coal stores, then put out to sea again. Because the old man was half-crazy worrying about the people who must be starving back home in the Old Country. And he had a cargo of frozen mutton under hatches.

But now one ruined city was much like another, even if it was London. Meanwhile, Fis and the captain were engaged in an animated conversation.

The ray had done its job thoroughly—wiping out metal as far west as Hawaii. "The Kanakas will come into their own," said the New Zealander, with satisfaction. "They were Stone Age before we found them, and now they'll just go back to being Stone Age again."

"And New Zealand isn't touched?"

"It didn't go that far south. New Zealand and the Falkland Isles are all that is left of the British Empire, except for the weather stations on South Georgia in the Antarctic. We met a Russian whaler who said that Kamchatka must have survived, because they'd picked up a radio message from there…"

The pontoon bridge rose in sight. "Anchor in midstream," said Fis. "And row ashore."

Then they looked astern.

Coming slowly, gingerly up river, hauled by a team of dray horses from the bank, was the magnetic survey ship, *Silva*. In her rigging, groups of men who were obviously inexperienced were trying to bend her sails.

And her decks were crammed with fierce-looking warriors. Gold swords and armor gleamed. They were heading north to revenge the death of their comrade who had fallen to the ship captain's pistol.

"Those are the gangsters I told you about," said Fis.

"They are afraid that, with the help of your ship, the Government will be able to mop them up. So they're going to fix you."

"Fix me, are they?" asked the New Zealander. "Hey, Joe—here are the keys of the gun case. Bo'sun, give out the guns as far around as they will go. You...Aussie...go below and fossick around in the hold until you come across that gunpowder harpoon we traded for meat from the Russki whaler."

"Aye, aye," Aussie replied.

The sailing ship was coming nearer.

"Landlubbers," grunted the New Zealander, between his teeth, as he saw the clumsy way the Nobs and Spivs were handling their craft.

The Captain gave out a motley assortment of weapons. A Webley, which had once been used by the Captain's Anzac father on the beaches of the Dardanelles. A .22 rifle kept for potting birds astern when the voyage got dull. A shotgun which had last been used on a shark. And the Captain's own pistol.

The *Manukau*, though a rusty old tramp, was the best-armed ship of war in the Western Hemisphere.

"Shall we give them a warning shot?" asked the bo'sun.

Just then a volley of hurled stones thudded across the deck. One near miss sent the Captain's cap spinning.

He turned around with red and angry face.

"Warning? Heck, no. Blast some sense into them."

The first volley, amazingly enough, caused complete panic on the deck of the sailing vessel *Silva*.

Many of the men aboard her were old soldiers. But they had finally got used to the absence of metal. The roar of small arms fire at close quarters (with no chance to retaliate) frightened them as much as it frightened jungle natives when they saw and heard firearms for the first time.

"Give them another," said the New Zealander, curtly.

The bowmen on the *Silva* were firing arrows, with burning straw dipped in tar twisted around their shafts. Several fell short and dropped hissing into the river. But one or two dropped on deck.

"Fire party! Ship's carpenter!" barked the Captain. And those men who were not armed busied themselves with buckets and reels of hosepipe.

"Setting my ship afire!" The Captain ground his teeth with rage. Then shouted, "Get a move on with that harpoon."

It was a good harpoon that could fire a pound-and-a-half explosive charge a couple of feet into the blubber of a whale, and then blow the creature out of the water.

An old seaman came forward and said, "I worked three seasons on the whalers, captain." There was a gleam in his eye. But the Captain said, "You go to Hades, old Tom. D'you think I'm going to let anyone else have the sport? I'm going to sink that floating matchbox myself."

He rammed the charge into the harpoon-thrower, aimed and fired.

The charge missed the bows of the sailing ship by about six inches. From the *Silva* came a noise that was a cross between a jeer and a roar of defiance.

"Two more charges left," said old Tom, significantly.

"You go to Hades," said the Captain. He reloaded, and took careful aim.

But Fortescue, at the wheel of the *Silva*, showed that he remembered some of the lessons he had learned in the old days, during yachting week at Cowes. He brought the sailing vessel around. And this time the charge fell short, raising nothing but a shower of spray.

"Last charge," said old Tom, meaningly.

The Captain rubbed his cheek. "Oh, all right," he said. "You take that harpoon, and blow her out of the water."

The gleam in the old seaman's eye grew brighter, but his expression did not change. He spat over the side, and slapped the side of the harpoon.

"Below the waterline," the Captain reminded him.

"Aye, aye, Captain," he said.

The *Silva* was now broadside onto the stream of the Thames. The avoiding action that Fortescue had taken last time had meant that this time she was drifting and helpless, with no weigh on her.

The old man trained the harpoon, and waited. Everyone on the *Manukua* held his breath.

Several seconds passed.

Then the harpoon gun coughed. The harpoon itself sped across the surface of the Thames, and entered the water just before it reached the *Silva*. There was a sudden roar, and the whole ship jarred and reared up.

No vessel that had just been patched up for a trip upstream could survive a jolt like that. The *Silva* was sinking by the bows, and the Nobs and Spivs rushed off the deck, diving and jumping madly into the Thames, and striking out for the north shore.

"Good shot?" asked the old seaman, modestly.

"Good shot, heck," said the New Zealand Captain.

"You've sunk her plumb in the fairway. How am I going to get my ship out of here, without dynamite?"

CHAPTER SEVEN
Free Trips to Mars

BEFORE Fis left Da behind as hostage, women had been very little in evidence among the Reds.

The duchesses emptying slops were, of course, a figment of the imagination. There were one or two harassed-looking mums and wives, trying to darn socks with needles made of bone, or attempting to boil up a nourishing soup from peelings. But all the important work was in the hands of the men.

When he got back, the women appeared almost to be running things. Opposite Charlie Smith's tent was another. A table stood outside, and at the table was someone writing documents with one of the precious swan-quills.

Around stood not men soldiers but women soldiers.

And when the writer looked up, lo and behold, it was Da.

Drilling out on the field were two groups of women. One lot—new recruits—was hard at training with mops and broomsticks. The other group, having passed their initial training, had graduated to spears.

While explanations were going on between the New Zealander Captain and Charlie Smith, the women kept interrupting. Da herself didn't say much—she just sat back in her chair, with a slow, artful smile on her face.

Finally, Charlie Smith took Fis to one side.

"It's been terrible since you were gone. That wife of yours! No sooner was your back turned than she was up making a speech. She started by saying that where you came from, no women would be content to stand by while their husbands ran things their own way. She got them all worked up—"

"Now tell me frankly, Charlie asked, "where do you come from, Russia?"

Fis shook his head, slowly. "Mars" he said.

"Oh...of course..."

"Mars," he repeated. "We come from Mars. Ask my wife."

"I've asked her. She said the same."

"Then why not believe us?"

"You'll tell me next that they speak English on Mars."

"Some of us do. I've been studying the Earth for the past thirty years."

Charlie Smith's eyelids flickered, but there was no other visible sign that he disbelieved this last incredible statement. Instead, he asked, softly, "How old are you, then?"

"Fifty." Charlie looked at the young man's smooth face, thick hair, erect stance.

"Any vacancies up there?" he asked, sarcastically.

But Fis continued seriously, "At the moment we've no means of getting back. However, if they send out a relief mission..."

A sudden ear-deafening noise stopped Fis from finishing his sentence.

At that moment, something landed on the tennis courts with a horrible smack. No one had looked up to see it coming, but when it landed abruptly, people scattered everywhere. A minute or two later, a hatch opened, and out of the space vehicle stepped the Chairman of the Elected Global Brains, panting slightly as his lungs adjusted to Earth's atmosphere.

To the Reds encamped in Battersea Park, the arrival of the New Zealand ship was completely incredible. They had adjusted themselves to a world in which there was no metal. They had quickly gotten accustomed to the thought that there would never again be steel ships crossing great oceans. And then, suddenly, the New Zealand flag waved once more in the River Thames. But the arrival of a Martian spacecraft was an even bigger incredibility.

Fis turned to Charlie Smith with a smile. He at least was one Earth dweller who was flabbergasted.

"Allow me to introduce," he said, "the Chairman of our Government."

The Chairman held out his hand a bit gingerly. It was plain that he, like most other Martians, still regarded the men of Earth merely as a highly developed species of animals.

"Mister Smith was just saying," Fis said, "how much he'd like to visit Mars."

But just as Charlie Smith was going to make a polite reply, one of the Reds came hurtling across the park toward his leader, shouting: "The bridge! The bridge!"

Da grabbed her spear, and ran to join her band of armed women.

"Don't tell me," said the Chairman, checking her, "that you're going to do anything so barbarous as to kill people with that instrument?"

Da shook herself free. "Don't you understand?" she asked urgently, "they're coming over the bridge. If we don't act quickly, they'll get in here and wipe us out. Any chance of planning life, and doing the planting that is needed, will have gone—"

"It seems you've become quite conditioned to Earth ways," said the Chairman, gently. And then Da realized this fight was nothing to do with her. She was a spectator. She was a scientific investigator. She was a different species.

"At least," said Fis, taking the Chairman with one arm and Da with the other, "let us see how this last battle goes before we desert them."

And taking from his belt his sword—still stained with blood—he handed it to a passing soldier.

Then they went to the riverbank and found a spot under the trees near the ruins of the former power station, where the pontoon bridge could be clearly seen.

The bridgehead was now securely in the hands of the survivors from the sunken *Silva*. And as they watched, they could see the first Nob infantry advance across the planks placed on the pontoons.

There are different sorts of courage, and perhaps the most desperate is that based upon despair. The Nobs were experienced with such despair. They and theirs had ruled for generations. It was especially hard for them to see power slipping from their grasp simply because they had been unable to adjust themselves quickly enough to radically changed conditions.

The first blow had been when the Spivs mutinied.

The Spivs didn't care much for this desperate fighting—all hard knocks and no loot. And they cared even less for the discipline. Fortescue had executed the Spiv who had let Fis escape—in front of all his comrades. And that had been the pretext for their mutiny.

Taking a few key Nobs as hostages, the Spivs made a fighting retreat from the Tower and headed east. After being pretty much mauled by guerillas from the Red East End, they finally retreated into the Essex countryside, where they planned to set up a black market in farm produce.

Fortesque's second mistake had been to treat the New Zealand ship as an enemy. It had cost him the *Silva*, and the support of many who earlier had trusted his judgment. When the survivors from the *Silva* had scrambled up out of the Thames, they were dissatisfied and desperate men.

There had been a brief dispute on some minor question between Fortescue and his second-in-command. A stabbing sword flashed, and Fortescue himself fell to the ground—to take no further interest in the art of warfare.

Yet Fortesque's abrupt death had served to rally the Nobs for one final battle. For unless they could cross that bridge and destroy the enemy camp, they had no future.

The attack came just as the bridge defenders' attention was distracted by the sudden flashing arrival of the rocket.

With a howl the Nobs charged forward.

Their first dash brought them so close to the bridgehead that there was only time for one fumbled volley from the slingshots. Then the fighting became hand to hand.

The Nobs fought like wild beasts, like savages from desert or jungle. They seemed almost impervious to the pain of wounds. When they were disarmed, they fought desperately, valiantly, with their bare hands.

The Reds, taken off balance, fought back. But they were soon overwhelmed.

Then the advance party of the Nobs set off across the bridge.

On the far bank, the ranks of the Reds' men and women had stiffened, waiting for the attack.

Charlie Smith was in command, cool as a seasoned veteran. The Captain of the New Zealand ship, at his elbow, hissed, "Fire! Why the heck don't you chaps fire!" But Charlie waved him to silence. At thirty yards, every catapulted stone might find its mark. At fifteen, with marksmen like his, every single stone would strike home.

"Fire!" he said, finally. His voice rang clear.

Above the whistle of the hurled stones came the repeated bark of the Captain's pistol, fired point blank.

"Slingshotsmen—*down!*" shouted Charlie. The slingshotsmen fell back. Already, behind them, the spearsmen were gripping their weapons tighter.

"Spearsmen—lower! Charge!"

A squad of spearsmen ran forward, the golden or flint tips of their weapons held waist high, spiking the rushing Nobs, causing them to waver.

"Spearsmen—*down!* Swordsmen—"

They had rehearsed this maneuver many times. The men with spears—those who survived the clash—fell back. And there behind them was a triple line of fresh men with stabbing swords.

"Swordsmen—draw! Charge!"

And forward they came, their short stabbing swords held at the ready.

From his observation point in the trees, the Chairman said, "It's just like your ancient history, citizen Fis—"

"With a difference," Fis replied, as they turned and walked toward the rocket. "These men adjust themselves much quicker to new conditions than I thought possible. There's a much greater readiness to cooperate with their fellows and to lend each other a hand than is evident to us on Mars. In my considered opinion, the majority of the human race is all right— it can confidently be left to look after its own problems…"

Da, a half-pace behind them, suddenly stopped.

"Where are we going?" she asked.

Her face was stained with tears.

"Back to Mars, of course," said the Chairman, genially. "Your investigation is finished."

"Back to Mars," Fis echoed. "Of course, I've enjoyed it on Earth. Even the unpleasant bits had their own fascination. But after all, Mars is home—"

And now she was actually weeping, her body shaken by sobs. "I don't want to leave them," she said. "All those women—they look to me to lead them—"

And in answer the Chairman pointed to the pontoon bridge, where, with hair and garments flying, the women Da had aroused and trained were already speeding to the North bank in pursuit of the Nobs.

"They seem to be getting on all right without you," said Fis, as kindly as he could.

"And they still," said the Chairman, just a little boringly, "have a minimum of industry in places like New Zealand and Kamchatka. Enough to produce things like ploughs and spades—not enough for wasteful things like arms. They've shown a remarkable capacity for adjustment to new conditions. Remarkable. Almost Martian. And besides," he said, as he handed Da through the hatch into the new type spaceship, his eyes twinkling almost as if he knew he had been a bore, "if they get into too much of a mess this second time, we can always send a second expedition and straighten them out anew."

He went to the control board and adjusted a few knobs.

Everyone in Battersea Park and for miles around was so busy fighting they didn't see the flash as the rocket set off for Mars.

A week later, as Charlie Smith, now Lord Mayor of London, started planning a punitive expedition after the Spivs in Essex, hardly a soul could have been gotten to admit that Martians had been involved in the war at all. Why give credit to the Man from Mars?

THE END

If you've enjoyed this book, you will not want to miss these terrific titles…

ARMCHAIR SCI-FI & HORROR DOUBLE NOVELS, $12.95 each

D-51   **A GOD NAMED SMITH** by Henry Slesar
         WORLDS OF THE IMPERIUM by Keith Laumer

D-52   **CRAIG'S BOOK** by Don Wilcox
         EDGE OF THE KNIFE by H. Beam Piper

D-53   **THE SHINING CITY** by Rena M. Vale
         THE RED PLANET by Russ Winterbotham

D-54   **THE MAN WHO LIVED TWICE** by Rog Phillips
         VALLEY OF THE CROEN by Lee Tarbell

D-55   **OPERATION DISASTER** by Milton Lesser
         LAND OF THE DAMNED by Berkeley Livingston

D-56   **CAPTIVE OF THE CENTAURIANESS** by Poul Anderson
         A PRINCESS OF MARS by Edgar Rice Burroughs

D-57   **THE NON-STATISTICAL MAN** by Raymond F. Jones
         MISSION FROM MARS by Rick Conroy

D-58   **INTRUDERS FROM THE STARS** by Ross Rocklynne
         FLIGHT OF THE STARLING by Chester S. Geier

D-59   **COSMIC SABOTEUR** by Frank M. Robinson
         LOOK TO THE STARS by Willard Hawkins

D-60   **THE MOON IS HELL!** by John W. Campbell, Jr.
         THE GREEN WORLD by Hal Clement

ARMCHAIR SCIENCE FICTION CLASSICS, $12.95 each

C-16   **THE SHAVER MYSTERY, Book Three**
         by Richard S. Shaver

C-17   **GIRLS FROM PLANET FIVE**
         by Richard Wilson

C-18   **THE FOURTH "R"**
         by George O. Smith

ARMCHAIR SCIENCE FICTION & HORROR GEMS SERIES, $12.95 each

G-5   **SCIENCE FICTION GEMS, Vol. Three**
         C. M. Kornbluth and others

G-6   **HORROR GEMS, Vol. Three**
         August Derleth and others